KT-492-034

Please return/renew this item
by the last date shown.
Items may also be renewed by
Telephone and Internet.
Telford & Wrekin Libraries
www.telford.gov.uk/libraries

Lettice and Victoria

ABOUT THE AUTHOR

SUSANNA JOHNSTON is a former features writer for *Tatler*. Her books include *The Picnic Papers* (Hutchinson), *Five Rehearsals* (Chatto), *Collecting: The Passionate Pastime* (Viking), *Parties: A Literary Companion* (Macmillan) and *Muriel Pulls It Off*, *Muriel's Reign* and *Late Youth: An Anthology Celebrating the Joys of Being Over 60*, all published to great acclaim by Arcadia. Susanna is married, with four daughters and ten grandchildren, and lives in Oxfordshire with her architect husband.

Lettice and Victoria

SUSANNA JOHNSTON

ARCADIA BOOKS

Arcadia Books Ltd
139 Highlever Road
London W10 6PH

www.arcadiabooks.co.uk

First published by Arcadia Books 2013

ISBN 978-1-909807-22-8

Typeset in Arno by MacGuru Ltd
Printed and bound by CPI Group (UK) Ltd., Croydon CR0 4YY

Arcadia Books supports English PEN *www.englishpen.org* and
The Book Trade Charity *http://booktradecharity.wordpress.com*

Arcadia Books distributors are as follows:

in the UK and elsewhere in Europe:
Macmillan Distribution Ltd
Brunel Road
Houndmills
Basingstoke
Hants RG21 6XS

in the USA and Canada:
Dufour Editions
PO Box 7
Chester Springs
PA 19425

in Australia/New Zealand:
NewSouth Books
TL Distribution
15–23 Helles Avenue
Moorebank
NSW 2170

For Ruby Susanna Weatherall, with Lola's love

Acknowledgements

Thanks to Karen Sullivan and my old, late friend
Percy Lubbock, who lived near Lerici in Northern Italy.

Part One

Chapter 1

Victoria's job was in Italy. Her mother, a tipsy invalid, lived in London and Victoria visited her as and when she was able to afford it. It was the second time she had travelled to and fro during her year of isolated employment. She knew the sort of night she was in for.

Body tilting sideways, dragged by the weight of her reclaimed suitcase (she had lost it once in Dover), Victoria boarded the train in Paris – bound for the South.

No need for bribes; it was not the holiday season and there was no competition for couchettes. The night ahead was to be long and the compartment, although designed for six hori-zontal travellers, was occupied by two others only. A mother and child. They were tentative; maiden voyagers. The mother, a weary Italian woman, cared kindly for her little girl who sat motionless – buttoned and bonneted. When the bonnet was removed, slowly and with gentle handling – bow untied with innocent skill – Victoria saw that the child, six years old at least, had not a hair on her head. It was completely shiny – veins on show. Her eyes were enormous, surrounded by navy shadows; pale cheeks swollen and furry. The whole body was unnaturally fat.

All three lay quiet as they journeyed. From time to time the mother rose and answered needs. In the morning, as the train drew up at the first station after crossing the border into Italy, loud and compelling voices shouted down the length of the platform, '*Café, panini, banane.*' Men with trays strapped to their shoulders handed pink, paper parcels in through the train window in exchange for coins or notes. As the three of them tackled their breakfast parcels, Victoria learned more about her companions.

The child was dosed with cortisone. Hair had fallen out and body had swelled. Friends and relations, backed by initiative from the parish priest, had paid for them to travel in search of help. A Paris doctor, renowned for curing, had offered them a free consultation, had written out prescriptions and given advice. Now they must bide their time.

There came a doubt, a hiccup, in Victoria's maternal yearnings.

Chapter 2

Alfredo, the butler, met her at the station. Oleanders were in bloom. The air was full of sun and the welcome was unqualified. Elena, a maid with odd eyes – tiny slits that cascaded with puss – crushed Victoria into embraces. Into her hands were pressed six sea horses; dry, perfectly formed, hard and curving. Elena's '*fidanzato*' Dante, a hunchback, picked them up each morning on the shore. There were tales to be told. The weather had been treacherous and Dante had been much thwarted by it. The cook, as usual, was a fiend but the *signorina* must wait for more details.

The *padrone*. He had been impossible. The *signorina* was to go to him at once. He had expected her the day before and had become impatient. She knew that to be unfair and untrue. He always tried it on.

Leaving her case for others to handle, she walked across the cool brown marble hall – first peeping into her luxurious bedroom. She was glad to be back, but frantic with fear of loneliness. How was she to meet a husband here?

In spite of the sickly child on the train her maternal instincts were still strong. The marble basin in her room, brownish orange like the hall, was enticing as was the four-poster bed – festooned in white mosquito netting. The sight of the bedroom refreshed her return and gave her hope.

The *padrone* was stationed, pampered but alone, in an upstairs room. His gargantuan, exposed stomach filled the scene. A tight silk dressing gown fell apart and a plaid rug slipped, leaving his belly bare. Nobody knew the truth about his eyesight but he led his life as a blind man. Shelves, covering each wall in the room, bulged with books, and from two windows the view down a terraced slope was of the sea – a sort of bay, mountains beyond. The ashes of his wife, long dead, filled an inch of a transparent urn on the mantelpiece – lidded and sealed. His mauve, podgy feet spilled over the sides of velvet slippers and the neck of a bottle glinted from under his armchair.

How did he collect and conceal bottles – blind as a bat? On a small mahogany table, near to where he sat, was planted his official ration. A carafe of warm and vinegary white Elba wine stood beside a glass and a plate of sugary biscuits, and his round face flopped into the folds of his chest as it fell forward.

Jerking it upwards as Victoria approached, he asked, 'Is that you?' He lifted a clean and little-used hand in greeting. 'You're late. We expected you yesterday.'

She had to shout. He was slightly deaf. It was tiring, raising her voice.

'No. It was always today. How are you?'

The last thing he wanted to hear was of her time away. Outside interests were forbidden. There was a backlog to be dealt with: letters, papers, books to be read. His nephew had written to him and Victoria had carried the letter with her from England and had nearly lost it with her suitcase – that and a silk dressing gown, sizes larger than the one Laurence wore.

In a voice trained to reach the hard of hearing, she read the letter aloud to him. 'Dear Uncle Laurence, I gather from Victoria that a new dressing gown might be an appropriate present so I send you one, using her as courier. I enjoyed meeting her when I handed the parcel over to her in London and I'm glad you have her living with you. Don't let her escape. It's not easy providing you with amanuenses at this distance.'

Had the nephew forgotten that she had to read letters about herself, trapped in captivity, aloud and at concert pitch?

She handwrote the one that Laurence dictated in reply.

'Yes,' he said, 'I'm lucky to have Victoria. Have no fear. She has promised to stay with me for ever.'

She didn't want to have to write that.

Not to admit on paper that she had no future. That she was to live for ever in a marble palace overlooking a remote bay in a foreign country, reading turgid volumes aloud, straining her voice.

'Laurence.' She spoke very loud, 'Not for ever. That was never agreed.'

'Well,' impatiently, 'say for a very long time. That will do. Say that. For a very long time.' The matter dealt with, they turned to Froude's *Life of Carlyle*. Victoria was only twenty. Laurence over eighty. Dickens in the afternoon, Walter Pater at teatime. Laurence was an admirer of Pater and called upon Victoria to halt from time to time as she read to him from slow-moving works. 'Take account of him, my dear. "To burn always with this hard gem-like flame to maintain the ecstasy is success in life." Not always easy, but advice worth following. "Get as many pulsations as possible during the given time."'

Laurence did not look as if he had ever experienced a single pulsation or, indeed, any moment of ecstasy. Nor did Victoria pulsate as, later, they listened to Mahler, massive and military, from a scratchy gramophone record on the terrace – Laurence permanently egg-bound and slightly drunk. He insisted on an egg dish at every meal.

Elena brought Victoria a breakfast tray the following morning. Strong coffee, a small circle of dry toast and apricot jam. Then she told of the cook's treachery; rationing her underlings and ladling out unfair burdens of work. Dante was not allowed to enter the kitchen any more. The cook said he smelled of fish. 'But, *Signorina*. He is a fisherman. How is he to earn his living?'

When Laurence had been placed, decent in the new dressing gown, on his chair by a twice-daily summoned male nurse, Victoria read the newspapers to him. They were airmail editions and always out of date. Firstly they had to be scrutinised. Laurence had fine feelings. The morning always started with a joke.

'Any rash engagements?' as she unfolded *The Times*.

Then, 'Any interesting deaths?'

Often she came under fire for her, in Laurence's pedantic view, mispronunciations.

'How about this, Laurence? *Schizophrenic* girl attacks *Eros*?'

His clean hand shot up.

'Two,' he said, pained and puzzled. 'Two mistakes.' Both words, schizophrenic and Eros, had been given the wrong emphasis.

'Women. Oh dear. Oh dear.'

Then, fearful of having in any way rebuffed her, he sometimes handed out a treat. Fishing in a fold of the dressing gown and bringing out a vast, round watch-face. 'Did I ever tell you what it was that dear Henry James said when he gave me this on my twenty-fourth birthday?'

'No, Laurence.'

He said, 'Dear boy. If you knew how cruel you were to be twenty-four – you wouldn't be it. You wouldn't be it.'

Almost shyly he signalled to her to open a drawer in his desk. 'Top drawer. On the right. A pile of letters from dear Henry. A long time ago.'

Also almost shyly, she went to the desk. A stack of letters in an educated hand lay there, one on top of the other. As Victoria flicked through them, as fast as she knew how, she noticed that each letter began '*Carissimo Ragazzo*'. Could it be that Laurence had ever qualified as such?

She picked one out and handed it to Laurence. He handled the priceless treasure and asked her to read the first line to him. She omitted the '*Carissimo Ragazzo*' bit and told him that it referred to one of Henry James's visits to America.

Laurence smiled very knowingly and, setting the letter down on his huge stomach, said, 'Dear Henry was on a visit to New York. I remember it well. In that letter he told me that he had been entertained, I think, at the Century Club, by a group of young people. He became aware that at the end of the room there was an easel that held a painting hidden under a sheet. Poor Henry. He realised that they were going to present him with it. Go on. Find the place. Read aloud to me what he said.'

Victoria strained to find the right page. The letters were long.

She arrived at the relevant place and read, 'It was unveiled and revealed a nudity of the most pronounced variety. What could I do? I couldn't leave it behind for fear of offending the young people. Had I taken it home, my housekeeper (Mrs Paddington) would realise that her worst suspicions were true. She'd realise that my reasons for this trip to America were dissolute ones.'

Laurence gasped in contentment and seemed to sink into his past.

Victoria put the latter back in the drawer with intention of reading more to him if and when Laurence allowed.

But he changed the subject swiftly, swore that he was a communist and that, all considered, a coffee-coloured baby was a delightful thing and that, unfortunately, Thomas Hardy wrote very badly but that he enjoyed the little twists in the novels of Agatha Christie. He had known her well in the past.

Occasionally he would refer to his own works. Then he'd chuckle. 'Balzac,' he said once, 'do you know what I wrote about Balzac?'

'No, Laurence. I fear I don't.'

'*Balzac was incredible but his taste was abominable.* I actually said that in print. It agitated many readers. It was a long time ago, of course.'

What a fix to be in. And she was very young.

Chapter 3

Victoria thought back over her reasons for being there in the first place. Stony-broke, on a frugal and protracted holiday in Rome, unable to survive by giving the odd English lesson, she had been defeated. She knew she must return home – but what then? Sharing her sickly mother's cramped quarters; typing in a pool or something. Her mother didn't miss her. She managed well enough, tottering to the public house at opening time, barely eating as much as a Scotch egg and returning with a lurch, cross and confused, to the slippery head of a kipper in the kitchen.

One evening in Rome, Victoria met a man at dinner. She had made friends with a group of English journalists who had asked her to join them at a trattoria. The man she sat next to was sixty or so, very sympathetic with tufty hair and soothing clothes; tweedy and well worn. She poured everything out; her fear of returning to London, her pressing indigence. How might she set herself up in Italy – untrained and ungifted as she was? More than anything she wanted to paint watercolor landscapes. Her talent was tiny, she told him. James Morton wrote her telephone number down on a paper napkin and said he would sleep on her conundrums. In the morning, he rang and promised to collect her in an hour. There might be a solution. Not necessarily a hundred per cent satisfactory one and with no guarantee that it would 'come off' but she stood a chance.

She bundled down the dirty stairway at her lodging house in the mood for inducement.

Driving northwards from Rome, James outlined his plan.

'I own a large and unmanageable castle about six hours from here, near the coast. An albatross. It will be a long drive. I have to go there to sort out problems. There are many, I can tell you. I fear it will have to be sold. It belonged to my grandmother. At present I rent it out for most of the year, but rent doesn't bring in enough to cover the outgoings and I can't charge my tenants much – it's too dilapidated.'

That was good. They were both hard up – or rather both had money worries.

He planned that she spend that night at his albatross from where he was to make telephone calls.

Nearby, in style, lived an old blind man. A man of letters. Victoria had never heard of him since he was known only in rarefied circles.

His way of life depended upon his having an Englishman living in the house to act as amanuensis, to read aloud to him and to write his letters. James Morton put emphasis on the word Englishman. No woman had ever held the post. Laurence Bland was reported to be a misogynist despite much weary pining for his wife, long dead. She had, according to James, been a frightful handful. Early in her life she had married a very rich man who had expired young, leaving her with one daughter. Later she married the writer Godfrey Slate who came to loathe her and who was a dirty word in Laurence's vocabulary. Nonetheless, he liked to draw attention to a late edition of Slate's *The Reality of Humanism* which, in the preface, quoted an earlier reader. 'I have read your book thirteen times and find it tiresome.' Now, Laurence was known to be desperate with loneliness on a promontory overlooking the bay where Shelley drowned. Anyone would do. Short-term maybe. James advised Victoria to give it a try. Living free, pocket money provided and plenty of time to paint the magnificent landscape. The perfect spot.

Laurence Bland never went near a telephone and James was uncertain as to whether his message had been delivered as they set out the following day.

Blue buses honked around curves, horns in constant use – so sharp were the bends. The villa stood high above a fishing port, not far in distance but interminable on the twisting ribbon of a road. Victoria felt sick, notwithstanding James's driving which was steady and cautious. Apprehension played a part. Also she had woken that morning with toothache; threat of an abscess forming above an upper tooth, near the front. She had no painkiller and no nerve with which to ask for one in this world of ageing men. The gum throbbed rhythmically as a painful pulse. Sneaking a glance in the driving mirror, she saw that her right cheek was puffy. James Morton laughed.

'Don't worry about your appearance. That's the least of your problems. Laurence won't be able to see you – but, if he could, he would be much pleased.'

Mortified at having appeared vain, Victoria came near to confession. On the other hand, to arrive like this with tooth-ache would be to let her well-wisher down. She had to stick it out.

The car had to be wrenched around to enter a drive that passed a lodge half-hidden in drooping wisteria. The flowers were pearly white; drop earrings for a giant's floozie. Victoria had never seen anything like it. Then the drive to the house – precipitous, downward sloping – rounded on a curve to the front of the villa leaving paths leading to the sea on the left. It was July and the bay was calm. Ilex and olive trees gave light to the entire space; acres of it. Silver glinted from leaves.

Elena, the maid, was standing there beside a lemon tree planted in a terracotta tub and bowed with bitter fruit. Cascades of verbiage preceded them as they crossed the threshold. The *padrone*. He had, indeed, expected *Signor* Morton but had given them the impression that he was to be accompanied by a *signorino*. And here was a *signorina*. The *signorina* followed, face in a spasm, the reddish dot still showing on her right cheek. A teething baby. Fortunate she wasn't dribbling. It was very hot, even for July.

They were led up a wide stairway and she was in a state of wonder at the shady beauty of all around her.

Then they were there, in Laurence Bland's study. He held his hand high in greeting.

'My dear James. You bring me help, I hear. I am most grateful. Where is he? I didn't catch his name. Introduce me.'

James approached and neared the chair of the misinformed host as Victoria hung back.

'Laurence. The message was incorrectly conveyed. I have a young lady with me. Victoria. Victoria Pattern.'

'I don't think that will do at all. Dear me no. Not at all.'

'Wait for a bit. She's prepared to act as stopgap. Help you with letters and so forth – even if you don't care to be read aloud to by a woman. I'm certain she can be of use.'

Victoria stood by the door – face inflamed, under discussion.

Egg mousse for luncheon on the terrace. Alfredo, the surly butler, attended with a smile of triumph on his lips. They were enjoying the joke – he and the cook. A young lady indeed!

Victoria tried to talk, exclaiming on the beauty of the place, shyly and in agony. Lucky it was mousse and slipped down past the abscess.

James talked Laurence into taking her on pro tem.

After lunch she was shown to her bedroom. Her few possessions were with her and with the help of Elena she laid clothes and oddments on empty shelves. Elena, ecstatic to have female company other than the cook's, attached herself with zeal.

James Morton departed, wishing her luck with a pat on the back.

That evening she ate alone with Laurence on the terrace. The ache in her face was harrowing. Elena had come up with some yellow pills and Victoria had swallowed a cluster as she hoped for the best. Dinner was as bad as could be. Alfredo, wearing white gloves, crept around the table and Laurence, willing the venture to flop, did nothing to encourage talk but picked at his omelette with a pearl-handled knife as a vast clay Buddha, not unlike himself, watched with blank eyes from above a tortoiseshell cabinet. She decided to make a determined effort the next day when definite duties might be laid out; letters and so on. How perfect it was in other ways. Landscape and architecture. She wanted to stay for a while – to live free in a beauty spot with time to take stock.

As she went to her room she overheard Laurence shuffling towards his own. He gasped and muttered, 'She won't do at all. Hopeless. No idea. Absolutely no idea whatsoever.'

Victoria dipped a flannel in cold water, pressed it to her cheek and lay down on the four-poster bed.

Chapter 4

Apart from the beauty and luxury of the place, the first few days, for Victoria, were ghastly. At least the toothache had subsided – perhaps assuaged by the yellow pills.

Each morning, when she took up her duties in the near-shuttered room to wait for the morning post to be brought in on a pewter tray by Elena, Laurence did no more than groan as he sat blinking and as his mauve feet spilled over velvet slippers.

Every weekday they awaited a crinkly airmail edition of the London *Times*, letters from Laurence's younger relations and on Wednesdays a copy of Sir Stephen King Hall's pacifist newsletter – with every syllable of which Laurence (who had been a conscientious objector during the war) agreed.

One morning a letter came for Victoria – addressed in an unknown hand. It arrived with the pacifist pamphlet and she had to put it aside and get on with Laurence's correspondence.

Once in her own room, she opened it. It came from her new friend, James Morton, the one who had landed her in it.

She read it absorbedly, again and again. 'My dear Victoria. Since I got back to England I have been feeling very apprehensive about your possible plight. Believe me, I would more than fully understand if you had already left. Laurence can be prickly and negative – also extremely spoilt. If, however, you are sticking it out, I have decided to give you a few tips!

'Laurence likes to talk of his wife. I imagine that you, with much justification, may have been fighting shy of the topic. She was a fiend and he worshipped her. It was, I imagine, a *mariage blanc* – Laurence having always preferred gentlemen to ladies and neither of them having been young when they married. She, Lady Sylvia (very important to remember the Lady bit), inherited a large fortune from her first husband. It's thought that she roped Laurence in when Godfrey Slate – her second husband – could stand no more of her. I once heard of a scene in a church in Florence where a memorial service was being held. Halfway through it Lady Sylvia whimpered, "Godfrey. I'm going to faint." Whereupon he shouted, "All right, Sylvia. Faint if that's what you want."

'She and Laurence came to the bay just after the war – having spent much of it in Switzerland – to the newly built house where now, perhaps, you still are. It's rumoured that Lady S. actually caused Laurence to lose his sight by insisting he read to her far into the night by the light of a pencil torch (anything brighter brought on one of her headaches).

'One night, so it's said, she was aggravated by the noise of a dog barking by the shore and sent Laurence out to have it shot.

He, of course, pacifist and aesthete that he is, had no gun and had to rouse the gardener to do the job for him.

'I tell you all this to amuse you and also to suggest that you ask him about Sylvia. It might work magic. Affectionately, James.'

She took James's advice that evening at supper. 'Tell me, Laurence, did your wife like you to read to her?'

He started, brightened and smiled. He took to her and she stayed on – almost the first woman, apart from domestic helpers, since the death of his hallowed wife, to penetrate the celibate sanctuary in years.

His stepdaughter came occasionally for a night to make sure that everything went well on the estate – destined to belong to her. The visits used to frighten Laurence into long silences for she was a formidable creature with a gigantic brain, a gigantic nose and very expensive clothes. She, Primrose, had married an Italian count and lived way south in Tuscany. She treated Victoria graciously as she might have done an invaluable servant whose notice she wished to avert. She praised her for her inner resource and increased her pocket money.

Occasionally the telephone rang. If the call was an English one, Victoria was summoned to deal with it. Laurence had long since given up the use of gadgets and was shaved each day by the male nurse. Sometimes calls were hard to deal with. Many pilgrims wanted to visit – Laurence having become an institution as a grand old man of letters living in a sensationally beautiful place – and calls were severely filtered.

The voice of an elderly man on the line. 'Can you tell Mr

Bland that I am in the neighbourhood? Hobson. Arthur Hobson. Two of us. We'd like to pay our respects.'

She ran and explained to Laurence that Mr Hobson waited for an answer.

'Arthur Hobson. He's a terrible bore. I like her. Caterina. She once gave me an alarm clock. Tell them to come to lunch – any day.' Unusual for Laurence to prefer a wife to a husband.

The day came and as they waited Laurence told Victoria, 'Arthur is a very limited man but – Caterina. You will enjoy Caterina.'

Disguised eggs – soufflé, mayonnaise and meringues, were prepared by the cook – Elena doing the donkey work.

Victoria greeted the guests on the doorstep. This had become one of her duties, for Laurence liked things to be done stylishly. The visitors arrived on time at a quarter to one.

Arthur Hobson, in his seventies, dapper in Sunday summer white, came forward. He wore a moustache.

'May I introduce you to my companion. Miss Lewes.'

Miss Lewes was American and many years younger than her protector. Not more than forty-five, Victoria guessed. Very dressy. It was lucky that Laurence would not be able to see her in her bright colours.

The alarm clock given to him by Caterina was wound up and ticking. Elena had scuttled about in Laurence's bedroom until she discovered its hiding place. She set it correctly, squinting through slits, and placed it beside the Elba wine and sugary cakes.

Laurence threw up his hands.

'My dears. I draw your attention to a priceless object. It is always here – at my side. As you know, I cannot see, so the pleasure of hearing your present tick is a heightened one. Come closer.'

Victoria went to him.

'Laurence. Mr Hobson is here with Miss Lewes. I don't think you have met her before.'

'What's that? Not Caterina? Oh, dear me no. That won't do at all. Tell him that won't do at all. Tell him some other time.'

Miss Lewes was aghast. It had been her idea. She had put pressure on her elderly lover to introduce her to the man of letters. The lover was knock-kneed, unmanned; wished he hadn't shown off about his acquaintances.

'Laurence,' he advanced towards the seated form of the blind man. 'Laurence. Miss Lewes is an admirer of your works.'

Laurence gave in with no grace and speeded up the arrival of lunch. It was served on the arched terrace, immediately outside the upstairs sitting room looking across rocks to the sea. Alfredo, white-coated, carried the food from the bowels of the house. That had become one of the cook's many bugbears. Since the *padrone* had been confined to one floor, soufflés flopped on the stairs.

When the guests departed with minimum farewells and 'another time bring Caterina' as parting shot, Laurence broke the lifetime habit of sticking to writing letters in the morning. He wanted to share his little bit of scandal and to send letters that very afternoon.

Together Victoria and Laurence tackled four.

One to a niece, two to nephews, and one to a correspondent in Northamptonshire.

'Imagine my surprise,' Victoria wrote four times. 'Not Caterina but a certain Miss Lewes…'

—— Chapter 5 ——

Laurence's crabbed lawyer came from Florence – all the way in a hired car with driver. Bernadini, he was called. Laurence ordered stuffed eggs and said that lunch must be on the dot. One o'clock sharp. Bernadini had been tipped off by the Contessa, Primrose, who had been worried by the state of financial chaos at the villa on one of her recent visits.

Laurence lived in dread of Bernadini. Blindness, though, came in handy. Victoria must deal with him. Discussions were to take place before lunch; eleven thirty, with Victoria taking notes. On the occasion of his previous visit to the villa the lawyer had warned Laurence that funds were running low. Were three gardeners really necessary with – 'how shall I put it? – the *padrone* chair-bound and unable to enjoy the sights and smells out there? Wouldn't one lad be sufficient?'

Then there was the indoor staff. Alfredo, the cook, Elena and Dante doing odd jobs. Couldn't Elena and Dante manage on their own now with the *signorina* living in and able to help with household matters; only the two of them to be fed?

Letters from the lawyer written during the six months between visits had been left unanswered. On this occasion Victoria greeted Bernadini and guided him across the hall, upstairs, past her own bedroom door to the sanctuary – ashes included. The nervy old lawyer steeled himself as Victoria stood by. He refused to sit but went up close to Laurence saying, '*Signor*. There is no money left. It has run out.'

'Run out? No. No. I felt sure there was enough for another fortnight.'

Eyes to heaven, the lawyer answered, 'It need not be a disaster, *Signor*, if you will kindly listen to me. Here you have a valuable property.'

So it was. Acres of sea frontage, olives and vines.

'One building – one only, perhaps one of the lodges – could be sold off separately for a large sum. Large enough to save the day.'

'If you say so. Perhaps we must. My wife would never have allowed it. My stepdaughter must be consulted.'

'She has agreed to it, *Signor*.'

Victoria guided his old soft hand over a provisional document prepared in advance by Bernadini. He had arrived full of pessimism but now there was hope. Laurence's blank eyes turned towards the urn on the mantelpiece.

—— Chapter 6 ——

As she opened the morning's post, Victoria's eye fell on a flimsy envelope; postmark English. Voice raised, she read it aloud.

'Dear Laurence (if I may call you this.) What an age since we met! Who are you, you may ask yourself. And well you might! Lettice. Lettice Holliday.' Bold italic hand and engraved daffodil telephone plugged into the paper. Relief nib dipped in mauve ink.

'Do you remember? But why should you? Lunch – on a lawn. Jugs of wine, straw hats, tennis. Yes! You've guessed! Tennis at the Lovelace's. Where have those days gone?

'And now a favour! My son, Edgar, can it be true? Oh, the tragedy of the passing of time! Yes! He's no longer a child! He will be in Italy (my wicked green eyes are glinting). Can he, might he, call on you? He works in the production department of one of the larger publishing houses. Bliss to be involved with books! They're sending him to Italy (then on to Yugoslavia – what it is to be young!) investigating printer's ink.'

Laurence winced and planned to say no.

Victoria, increasingly aware of her isolated position, was scared. Only the day before she had heard from a school friend asking if they could meet in Florence for a few days. Surely the old geyser would let her off the hook for the odd night? He only paid her a pittance after all. She had asked for permission to go but Laurence merely replied, 'Oh no. I don't think that would do at all. What would become of me? Oh dear no. It wouldn't do at all.'

Defeated, Victoria thought of novels she had read. *A Handful of Dust*. She was captive. Lettice's letter was in her hand.

'Let's give the absurd person's son a try, Laurence,' she found herself shouting. 'I'll see to the room and he might have news from London. Theatres or something.'

'Very well, but one night only.'

Soon after he had refused to allow Victoria to join her friend in Florence, Laurence was fearful of her displeasure and offered one of his rationed treats.

'Did I ever tell what dear Henry James said when introduced to a bevy of beauties? One of them was the celebrated actress Ellen Terry.'

He had told her twice but she answered, 'No, Laurence. What was it?'

'One of the miserable wantons was not without a certain cadaverous charm.'

Two weeks later, Victoria rested her elbows on the windowsill and squinted sideways to watch Edgar Holliday hop out of a hired car. He was handsome, as far as she could see, unexpectedly so. Lanky but trim. With a mother sounding like that Victoria had pictured a fright. She watched Elena greet him, washing him with words he couldn't follow. She waited in her room. The visitor was being led past her door by the slit-eyed maid, heading for Laurence's study, and she decided to join them there – efficient with her notebook.

Laurence introduced them.

'This is Victoria. You mustn't distract her during your short visit. We have work to do. I hope you'll find everything you need.'

Edgar, ignoring house rules, asked, 'But can I take her for a drive this afternoon? I'd like to do some sightseeing as I have a hired car and my free time is rationed.'

Laurence sank back and patted the new dressing gown several times.

During eggy lunch the matter was raised again.

'Very well. Very well. But bring her back for tea.'

The villa was remote and there were few sights of interest nearby. Victoria, stuck on the promontory as she had been, had seen little of the neighbourhood and hankered for an outing to a town on the edge of a lagoon – not impossibly far away. She had heard about it in a letter from a friend. Puccini's birthplace at Torre del Lago, near Viareggio. Beside the lake the maestro had been inspired to write *Madame Butterfly*. That was all she knew. Edgar made a dash to the car and returned with a fistful of maps. It was possible but tea would have to be scrapped. Laurence groaned and gave in.

Edgar was pernickety in the car, fussed over the tyres and

was unused to driving on the right. Victoria took charge of the route and read aloud from a guidebook. It described Puccini's house, now a museum, as 'enchanting'.

They left the car beside a restaurant in the square that, on one side, bordered a lake. The restaurant, enclosed on three sides by green verandahs, jutted out over the water. Lazy drinkers sipped in sunlight. The square was semi-tropical, planted here and there with palm trees and brightened by red geraniums stuffed into massive tubs. Umbrella pines spread, tops flattened, on the other side of the lake. Half-hidden in the greenery, Victoria spotted the hero. Puccini. Larger than life, wearing a thick overcoat, collar upturned, under a broad-brimmed hat. The statue, green and speckled, might have been modelled in lead; lead or copper. She wasn't sure which. A cigarette was stuck between his lips, tucked in under a waxy moustache. Perhaps he was wondering what next to compose. Perhaps marking down a local lass to share his bed that night. The sharp point of a handkerchief stuck out of his pocket at an impertinent angle. Edgar asked Victoria to stand beside the figure while he took a snap. She was tickled pink. Nearby there was a kiosk where souvenirs were sold. Miniatures of the swaggering statue, skimpy Madame Butterflys, cards, posters and the Pope's head converted into a battery lamp. From a restaurant drifted strains of potted Puccini taken fast on a jukebox. Surrounded by souvenirs (Christ in a shelly grotto, tortoises and crabs combed from the lake, models of Turandot encrusted with sequins), Edgar bought a postcard for his mother. Then a miniature maestro for a speechless Victoria.

She slipped it into her bag and felt disturbed. He asked for the museum, the one described as enchanting in the guidebook. A man smiled and pointed. There was something in his face that reminded her of her miniature maestro and all the other miniature maestros that stood shoulder to shoulder on the stall, as he wagged a finger towards iron railings a few feet from where they stood. A small group gathered there and waited beside a closed gate. Edgar and Victoria gaped through the railings at a modest villa. Beside the gate, moulded into the ironwork was a tatty, ill-connected bell. Under this, written shakily in pencil, they saw the word 'Puccini'. Perhaps he was in. A tall German woman, member of the group, stuck her finger on the button and a shrill ring came from the villa a few yards up the path, flanked by more geraniums in pots. A figure shuffled towards them – fat fist pointing outwards, keys on a ring in his hand. His signal demanded patience. Again Victoria noticed familiarity in a stranger's face. His clothes were shabby but his moustache was trim. He unlocked the gate and ushered them in. Bright art nouveau tiles lined the room. They showed willowy girls holding out bunches of lilies under a setting sun that shot out spiky rays. Victoria clasped her bag and the small statue that Edgar had given her. She was excited.

An attitude crisis attacked her. Edgar was nice enough – but was it because he was the only man to have crossed her path in months? Puzzled, lit up and aghast amongst treasures, she touched the legs of the maestro's piano and blinked in delight. There beside her was his aspirin bottle, his spectacles, his white and waxy death mask lying snug on the pillow where his true, living head had lain during final hours. A dedicated smoker he had died from a cancerous growth in his throat. Victoria decided to stop smoking now that things were looking up. Edgar stood beside her and made comments. He was enjoying himself, running a hand over a mother-of-pearl screen; a present to the maestro from the Japanese government to mark the opening performance of *Madama Butterfly*, as the guide called it. Behind the piano, bones of members of the Puccini family were walled up. All squeezed in somehow. The group filed past the family monument that held them tight and dead behind it; then into the gun room. Boots for every type of weather, macs, cartridge bags and guns took up most of the space. The visitors could hardly inch in and Edgar's body was close against Victoria's. Victims of sport in glass cases stared out to the lake – expressions curiously forgiving. A great crested grebe, two pheasants, a cormorant, tufted ducks. Edgar recoiled. His father was an ornithologist of acclaim. There was also an owl, beside it a bag or two of feathers and the odd loose wing. But a good set of antlers and a mothy deer's head cheered him up. Jammed tight, in corners of the room, were clusters of enormous guns and rifles; every shape and size.

Back in the main room where the tour had started, the guide took charge. He led them to a portrait of the great composer. It was surrounded by framed photographs and original manuscripts. He halted under the gilded frame, his concentration deep, and with a chuckle pointed to the face inches above him and almost identical to his own, '*Bel uomo.*' Identical, too, to the face of the souvenir seller. He explained with a shrug that his mother had been a serving maid in the house, his father the gardener. The disapproving face of Puccini's sister, Soeur Angelica, a nun in nun's habit, hung alongside. Victoria glanced at Edgar and wondered how much the nun had known of her famous brother's philandering.

The guide, in full swing, held forth again in faulty English, 'The maestro had four great loves and they came in this order. Smoking. Women. Shooting, Music. Music was the least in importance to him'

Hints of the guide's inherited lechery as Edgar stood by made her feel shaky and unsure. Shyness mingled with distaste and a modicum of desire confused and frightened her. Confused and frightened her even more, later, in the car park where many more Puccini lookalikes scampered in every direction. Edgar almost leering by her side.

—— Chapter 7 ——

In fear of Laurence's certain grumpiness, they drove back to the villa. Edgar told her that he had one more free day. If only Laurence would allow him to stay for another night, there might be the chance of one more sightseeing trip. He appealed to Victoria. 'I'm afraid I've made you late for tea but aren't you rather over-restricted?'

'I know. It's hopeless. I handle it badly. I'm awfully wet.'

'Perhaps I should visit you more often. May I?'

That evening Laurence, in his doubtful blindness, was unaware of conspiracy.

'I hate to introduce a sad subject,' he picked over his omelette, 'but what time do you have to leave in the morning?'

Her face was hot and her voice reached concert pitch as Victoria made her first stand.

'Laurence. Can Edgar stay for another night?'

'Very well but I can't have you distracted again. Tomorrow he will have to look after himself.'

Edgar had to go for a drive on his own during that day but in the evening he kissed Victoria at bedtime. Before breakfast the next morning he was on his way.

Both Victoria's mind and body were riddled with unedifying torment – agitation almost overpowered by mortification. She did not forget the kiss. That had almost been exciting. Professional if mechanical. Not that she found Edgar sensitive or full of heart. Far from it but might he do? In her thoughts for the future, nothing else was ever likely to offer. He liked her. He had kissed her. He had a job. He had a flat in London. She counted assets as she fell asleep.

There wasn't much doubt when, a week later, a letter stamped in Dubrovnic was handed to her by Elena.

'Nothing here to touch the magic of Puccini's lake. But then part of the magic was the company...'

He asked if he might return for a night or two on his way back. There was a chance of swinging it with his production department; printer ink in her neighbourhood might be of interest to them. Could she swing it with Laurence?

She lost her nerve.

Conspiring with Elena they booked him a room at a guest house further up the hill, and each night after Mahler, interminable on the terrace, she stole away and walked to the end of the drive where Edgar, having made his report on printing ink, waited in his hired car before driving her back to his *pensione*. She was shy and unnerved but allowed herself to be swept along.

During the first night there was a peculiar storm. To start

with, only lightning and wind; no rain or thunder. The lightning was pale and occupied the entire space of the bedroom window, occasionally flickering. It was not lightning as Victoria knew it. It had never been like that at any stage during her time at the villa. It was as if electricity had been turned on, powered by a faltering generator, to illuminate the sky. It was September and figs were ripe and splitting open. On a terrace outside the window of the *pensione* the wind whipped the sea and bashed at trees so that figs sploshed to the ground. A herd of cattle dropping tiny cow pats. Then came an assault on the eardrums. Dense and deafening thunder. A million buckets emptied from the sky. Amplified crackles; louder and louder. Edgar went to the window and Victoria wished her underclothes had not been threadbare. She kicked them under a chair. Window and doorframes were ill fitting and the room was bright.

They lay very close and he told her of his family; his gifted ornithologist father, his elegantly refined mother and the atmosphere of tasteful peace at the tower where they lived on the borders of England and Wales. By the skin of its teeth the tower was in England. It was all that remained of a mediaeval fortress half converted in Victorian times. The main floor of the tower was used as a darkroom. Above it and reached by a winding stairway in the thickness of the walls, were two floors used as overflow bedrooms in the summer – uninhabited in winter months. The rest of living was taken care of in the Victorian wing. Under the tower there was a dark vault housing home-produced wine, elderflower and dandelion syrups. Lettice and

Roland had bought it when the children were young and had renamed it 'The Old Keep'.

They planted lavender bushes and laid out brick paths leading to the riverbank. His mother, Edgar told her with some reverence, spent a lot of her time writing letters – inviting intellectual people to stay. Victoria had nothing to exchange with him – her mother, inebriated and wan, her only kin. She was in his bed, deprived of self-control, in a hair-raising storm in a shabby *pensione* on a piece of isolated coast and hearing tales of his home life. He spoke in a flat voice and, at fixed intervals, cleared his throat but Victoria revelled in closeness after the emptiness of her days and nothing else offered. She was hungry to belong to someone and didn't mind who. They indulged in violent passion. Edgar was twenty-six and balding slightly on top and near the back of his head. In London, he told her, he owned a basement flat in Battersea. She hungered to see it; kitchen, books and bedroom. Also the tower and the irreproachable parents. She thought of Lettice's absurdly affected letter and feared there might be a flaw in their unity of vision. Still. Mothers didn't matter. Thirsty for the opportunity and drunk with the chance to rescue herself from spinsterhood, she agreed to marry Edgar as soon as she could extricate herself from Laurence's grip. 'One day,' she told him, 'but I have no idea when that will be.'

'I'll wait,' he promised with a crooked smile and sadness printed on his face.

The next day, as she soaked in a marble bath, feet propped in front of her on a wooden rack, she counted her toes. Did she

own all ten of them, she wondered. Were they soon to become
the property of Edgar? Maybe one of them, the little one on its
way to market, would be kidnapped by his mother.

Chapter 8

How was she to break it to Laurence? How was she to find a successor? How was Edgar to break it to Lettice – to disturb the tranquillity of her dreamy days, poetry and flowers?

She came very near to funking it.

Begging her by letter, as he daily did, to return, Edgar barely touched on the matter of his family's reaction.

He suggested a secluded wedding; just the two of them and some sort of witness. Victoria was relieved. Her mother, scarcely capable of smiling let alone handling a celebration or being able to afford one, was off the hook.

Just then the poor tipsy thing became seriously ill overnight. A neighbour sent Victoria a telegram and she had, willy-nilly, Laurence or no Laurence, to return to London, Edgar or no Edgar. He met her at the station and loads fell off her back. A male companion acted as a painkiller.

Edgar behaved with masterly correctitude, seeing to details of death when the sad lush, destined never to become his mother-in-law, expired.

Notwithstanding his help during difficult days, Victoria already looked forward to returning to Italy and freeing herself again from Edgar. It hit her that no sooner had she escaped from her last type of captivity than she started to hanker to return to it.

She entered into the depression of mourning as she looked around her mother's flat. It was up three floors in a house on an outlying London street. Many stairs for a little drunk lady, whose name had been Lilias, to tread. It was very small – one bedroom, a dismal bathroom and a kitchen that consisted of no more than a sliced-off corner of the room. It was all, though, very neat and tidy. No empty bottles in spite of the alcohol that Lilias had poured daily into her small body. Several pairs of spectacles were neatly snapped into their cases. Very few sheets and towels were methodically stacked and shelves were clean. The emptiness made Victoria frighteningly sad.

The pair decided to spend some nights there as they arranged to have a few pieces of battered furniture removed to Edgar's flat in Battersea where they were to live after they were married. No souvenirs. No photographs of her as a child. Clothes, tinned soups and a near-perished hot-water bottle to be binned. Dangerous to use a hot-water bottle when drunk.

Edgar was respectful to Victoria and they both strained to re-enact the passion they had shared together in the thunderstorm by the sea. He was courteous and assured but did not refer to any earlier courtships. Perhaps he had patronised many a brothel. Something lacked and his limbs were abnormally cold, particularly in the early mornings. One evening he handed her an engagement ring. It had been supplied by Lettice – sent with a note to Edgar saying, 'For my firstborn to place on the finger of his lady love. I was given it by a disappointed suitor. I suppose I should have returned it but I'd already broken his heart and didn't want to rub salt in the wound.' Victoria didn't care for it. As far as she could make out, it represented the entwined symbols of art and music – a quill pen entangled with a lute or something.

Victoria had involved herself, once or twice and hurriedly before, with men but never to the extent of spending a night with one – or of making a promise to marry. She watched him as he undressed – near to her in the small room. He unhooked a stretch of cloth that went across the top of his trousers before undoing fly buttons, one by one. Zips were just coming into vogue but Edgar was old-fashioned. Why fly? Fly leaf? Something that's covered. Maybe they attracted flies. She disliked the flagrant attention paid to the penis's position. Women exposed no urges in their dress.

They moved, with the help of an odd-job man with a van, to Edgar's basement flat in Battersea. It turned out to be to her liking – having the bonus of a small garden at the back. The rooms were reasonably large and well furnished. Needlework pictures, a few Kelim rugs, pictures with maple-wood frames, some embroidered cushions, an upright piano with candlesticks attached. Probably all provided by his mother. There were, too, bird pictures painted by his father – skilled but spindly and lifeless. Edgar, with awkwardness, showed her round. There was a little room at the back of the flat where a cot would fit with ease. There might be a nursery school nearby. Limbs cold or not, she had made up her mind to marry Edgar. His limbs might get hotter. Her reason slipped in every direction.

One evening the telephone rang and Edgar signalled her to answer it. 'I hail and greet thee, my *belle fille* to be. Would that we could meet during your days in England. So very sorry about your dear mama. *The Way of All Flesh* – one of my very favourite books. I'm folded here in my canopy of moss and ivy and, mainly because of the hatefulness of our financial position, just cannot get to the metropolis for the time being.' She clearly found it a struggle to be picturesque as she returned to the topic of the engagement ring and the suitor's heart that she had broken. Victoria half listened as Lettice told of her hopes of a meeting. 'Edgar tells me that you will go back to the great man of letters for a spell. What a privilege to have dwelt in a literary environment. Books! We have far too many of course.'

Victoria hushed her, saying that she much looked forward to visiting The Old Keep – saying it as she yearned to be back amongst the olives, Laurence's dead wife's ashes, Elba wine, Elena, Dante and pine trees.

She had spent her life blocking things out. She had the knack. Somewhere she sensed shame but hid it from herself for she was curiously exhilarated by the prospect of new people (even Lettice), new places, a baby, a home, a kind man to trouble himself with her. She hoped not to trouble him.

From London, Victoria wrote to Laurence to explain what had happened and to say that there were things to be seen to and, desperately sorry as she was, she had to delay her return to the villa. Then, when she did return, it was only to be for a short time. She was to marry Edgar Holliday as soon as he, Laurence, was able to spare her. Meanwhile, she was searching high and low, but not too low, for a substitute and would return to her post for as many weeks as it took them to find a replacement.

For some reason, maybe because the situation almost suited her, Victoria had only faintly queried the motive for Edgar's speedy proposal of marriage. He barely knew her. It crossed her mind that he might have some vital cylinder in his make-up missing; had been underfed and stunted by his absurd mother. Something wonky in his outlook. Possibly he proposed to every girl he met. Possibly he had been rejected fifty times – or more. A misfit with stifled emotions. What didn't occur to her was to wriggle out of it.

Laurence, assisted by an English-speaking neighbour, replied to her letter, sending it, as planned, care of Edgar's flat.

'My dear Victoria. This has come as a terrible shock. Firstly, of course, I refer to the death of your dear mother. Then I come to a more serious matter. That of your intention to marry. I hope you are entering into this of your own accord; that you are exercising your own free will. You were, after all, very happy here. Are you under any unreasonable pressure? You know the rules, don't you? Twenty-four of everything. No young lady in my day would have considered anything less. Starting with twenty-four handkerchiefs. I look forward to seeing you here again as soon as possible and I, for one, believe in very long engagements.'

Before the inner myth that she had woven into herself

exploded, she went back to Italy with the ring on her finger and hoped that once she had a base with Edgar she would take proper painting lessons. Go to art classes; have a baby. Edgar was kind and said he loved her. Seeing her off at the station, Edgar outlined plans. He was to take out an open-dated, special licence and be there and ready to marry her as soon as she returned. He planned to explain to his mother that the wedding was to be private on account of recent death. Then there might be a party at Christmas time.

She fingered the ring.

Tears trickling through slits, Elena carried in the breakfast tray and clipped back mosquito nets around the bed although it was late in the season for such insects. So. The *signorina* was going to be married. To that handsome fellow she had spent nights with at the time of the thunderstorm. She and Dante had already waited for four years. Dante had suffered once more in the storm. It had been too rough for fish but more sea horses had been washed up. Shoals of them.

Laurence probed about in a velvet-padded box.

'I wish I could give you twenty-four of these,' he said, presenting a brooch; a shimmering stone once worn by his wife.

There were no more jokes about rash engagements.

Victoria meditated on her future and on Lettice's letter. The one telling of Edgar's very existence. It made her shudder. Her future husband, it seemed, took his mother seriously; a symbol of culture and polish. But a loving son was a good thing to be. Anyway, Lettice might not be as bad in the flesh as she was on paper. There might be a good heart beneath the furbelows.

Victoria sifted through a heap of letters in answer to various leads she had followed whilst searching for her replacement. A letter of recommendation came from the editor of a literary magazine. His name carried weight with Laurence.

'I write to introduce you to a young cousin of my wife's. Mungo Craddock. He is just down from Oxford and aspires to write. I think you would take to him. He is sensitive and a Roman Catholic convert. Some priest in Oxford got hold of him during his second year. He is a serious boy and a member of a large family. I think he would fit in. I urge you to give him a try.'

Laurence waved his much-waved hand.

'Roman Catholic convert! No. No. That wouldn't do at all.'

In other ways Mungo sounded suitable.

Although she was in no real hurry to leave, she knew that she must get on with plans and wrote to the young man – Roman Catholic convert or not.

Life there was, in many ways, ideal but it stood still as it waited for Laurence to die. His stepdaughter was, anyway, unlikely to have need of her there.

Mungo Craddock's well-mannered reply whistled back.

Chapter 9

It was late October when Mungo Craddock arrived. Victoria had promised Laurence that she would overlap with him for a week to show him the ropes.

Taking up a vigil at her window overlooking the porch, Victoria dug her elbows hard down into the crumble of stonework on the sill. She covered her face with both hands and squinted between cracks. Playing for time and willing it to pass, she clasped her fingers together and then quickly parted them again. Fleeting glances between bars brought a painful reflex. It reminded her of Edgar's arrival, not long before, at the same spot. The two events became interchangeable. Perhaps this new one would have done just as well.

Mungo Craddock arrived in Laurence's car, having been met by Alfredo at the station. Victoria widened gaps between fingers as he came into view. She whistled with relief. She had, after all, chosen the better favoured of the two. Edgar was, at least, presentable. It surely proved that she was not entirely omnivorous. A short young man, bespectacled, made himself known to Elena who waited by the lemon tub.

A beard tangled up in a watch chain reached his waist. Beard, tweed and watch chain. No nonsense about a language barrier. He had been up all night with a phrase book. Grin fixed, he advanced on Elena.

'*Buon giorno. Sono molto contento.*'

Victoria darted to her bedroom and heard them pass – wondering how on earth she was going to swing it with Laurence.

Victoria stole in behind them thanking her stars that, as with Mr Hobson's Miss Lewes, Laurence couldn't see him.

Mungo advanced upon his puffy future patron, Victoria and Elena waiting in the wings as Laurence sat – a pint of milk in the armchair – pale and sloppy, washed-out eyes shielded by spectacles.

'Mr Bland. This is a tremendous honour. I cannot tell you with what excitement one has anticipated this meeting.'

'Laurence. Please. I prefer to be called Laurence.'

'I say. That's frightfully good of you. What a delightful room.' Mungo looked about jerkily but didn't spot the spies.

'What an enchanting landscape.' He pointed at a picture propped on a table. It was one that Victoria had painted and mounted herself. A pointless present for a blind man.

Inwardly shrinking with anxiety, she made her presence noticeable and introduced the pair to each other.

As Laurence sipped, Mungo buttonholed her.

'Could you kindly put one in the picture concerning form here. One gathers that you know the ropes. One does want to strike the right note with the old dear. And by the way, about the maid. Is there something the matter with her eyes? Something one should know about?'

Elena whirled him away to see his quarters. Laurence had suggested that he might like to wash after his journey. Shave perhaps? Little did he know.

Victoria waited for a verdict but none came.

At lunch, refreshed by his wash but having taken no advantage of the shaving offer, Mungo pressed on.

'Might one be allowed to read one or two of one's short stories to you, sir?'

'Laurence, please. Call me Laurence.'

'Sorry. It's going to take a bit of getting used to. Laurence, I intended to say. It would be the most tremendous honour.'

'By all means. Indeed. Sometime.'

'They are inspired by Thomas Aquinas. By the way, Laurence, is there a Catholic church near here?'

Victoria was at sea. They were, after all, in Italy.

Chapter 10

Mungo had asked permission to go to a special mass in the village that morning so Victoria sat alone, gratefully, with Laurence in the shaded room – a small pile of letters to be opened on her lap. One was for her and, unmistakably, came from Lettice. Laurence had not quite finished his first glass of Elba wine and signalled that he was not ready to hear what his post had brought. She opened the one addressed to herself.

'Ma *belle fille* to be! I wish we could have lured you down to The Old Keep when you were in London but we knew time was precious for you and fully understood. Edgar has told us all! Your meeting in heavenly Italy – and it's partly my doing! What luck that I'd met the great man of letters (or are these things luck?). Warmest regards to him from all of us in our bosky retreat. How can you tear yourself away from such a fount of learning? Love conquers all! Families are such wonderful things and, knowing that you – poor darling – are an orphan, how we all long to gather you into the bosom of ours.'

Victoria tapped her foot and sang, loud and clear, an old ditty.

Now my mother-in-law is dead,
She got shut in a folding bed.

'What's that?' Laurence was disconcerted.

'Sorry,' she said, 'I was dreaming. What do you think of Mungo?'

She didn't give a fig either way at that moment.

'He's shy. Awkward. But, do you know? I rather like him.'

She felt a pang of rivalry – was she no longer indispensable?

'Do you know?' he said to her later. 'He read me some of his stories. One or two of them had something. He admires my work. All that was a long time ago.'

He was half asleep and she tiptoed back to her packing. Elena was there hoping to help and in tears. Things were certain to go downhill now with the *signorina* gone and that clown '*buffo*' all bewhiskered around the house.

Before she went to sleep she reminded herself of how once, when she had finally and timidly, told Laurence that she had been interested in something he had written in his youth, he had said, half smiling, 'Oh my dear. In the old days all we writers wanted were copious draughts of unqualified praise.'

The *buffo*, with his copious draughts, had revived memories.

She spoke to herself. 'If you're old and isolated, you like what you get. Perhaps Laurence knows he's stuck and he's going to make the best of it. That's what he did with me. Still,' she decided, 'he liked me best. I know it. Even if I wasn't much good at delivering unqualified praise.'

On her return to London Victoria married Edgar.

Part Two

Chapter 1

W hile Edgar's father, Roland Holliday, stood, field glasses in one hand, paintbrush in the other, his wife Lettice painted her own imagined picture of the opening of the London exhibition of his recent work that was soon to take place.

Sketches of birds and twigs stood propped in the hall.

The list of guests was too confusing a task to tackle during the day and best left for night hours. She snatched a flat flower basket from the garden room and walked down the gravel path to the spot where her husband stood. Her hand touched his arm. Wincing, protective of his brushstroke, he turned towards her.

'How many have you finished?' Her bony face was tip-tilted.

'Not enough. I think I'll have to put the exhibition off until next year. You can always bully a few friends into buying something from me between now and then.'

It must be that he was trying to torment her.

'Don't be absurd. The gallery could sue you. Of course you

can do it. I have always said it and I say it again, every creative artist needs to work to a deadline. You must stick to yours.'

Later, in the kitchen garden, she hacked viciously at the stem of a red cabbage.

That evening they ate a bleak meal. The purifying influence of homeliness for which The Old Keep was celebrated, deserted it when there were no witnesses. Casserole dishes and open fires kept for appropriate occasions lay in abeyance, sheltered by dust and ash as Roland submitted to the regular and dramatic changes that were made in their standard of living.

Five children had been raised there but now the couple was often alone. Their youngest daughter, Joanna, was still at boarding school but usually mucked about at The Old Keep during the holidays. Roland painted and studied birds as Lettice shuffled through her short list of weekend visitors. The one ahead was significant. Edgar and Victoria were to come for the first time since their quiet wedding.

Lettice was put out by Victoria's not seeming to be intellectual. Strange, having had that interesting job with the man of letters. She was already wearing the anxious look of a woman yearning for a child, smoked a great deal and it was rumoured, although opportunities at The Old Keep were too few to provide proof, was inclined to get tipsy. Scary bits of tittle-tattle concerning her late mother had filtered in.

It was lucky that she was pretty, for she certainly had no idea of how to dress. It seemed that she was not even interested in trying to look elegant, which was a shame – for Edgar's sake.

A middle-aged scholar, an old friend of the family, and a shy young professor were due to arrive on Saturday on their way to a reading party further west. The two were almost inseparable but Lettice believed there to be nothing improper in their relationship. She claimed them both to be 'brains of Britain – united by the majesty of their thoughts'.

Edgar and Victoria would be there on Friday evening so there was time to drop a tactful hint to Victoria, since Edgar was too dazzled by his bride to think there was need for advice.

Lettice selected books to place at her side of the bed.

'Darling. Do read that charming book. It's just down your street and dear Archie Thorne wrote the introduction so it will be fun for you to discuss it with him tomorrow.'

'Didn't you love it?' Victoria was asked in the morning.

'I don't think I understood it.'

'Isn't she modest, Edgar? Long may she remain so.'

Victoria knitted, lit a cigarette and wriggled as near to the fire as she dared. She had been cold since arriving.

'I love to see a young girl use her hands. Have you ever thought of embroidery? I think you'd find it more rewarding than knitting.'

'No. I never have.'

'Let's go together to the Women's Home Industries. I love a trip to London. So many friends to see. We could get those wonderful ladies to draw up an interesting design and I'd lend you the Regency stool from my bedroom to cover.'

Victoria wanted to ask Edgar to get her a drink. It was only eleven o'clock but the day was cold and wet. She made a sign but Edgar ignored it and wished that he'd been more robust when speaking to Victoria of his mother.

By Saturday afternoon, the flower basket was piled high with sodden roses. Loaves rose and swelled as Lettice decanted home-brewed wine.

Victoria felt sick and, hoping it might be an omen, went to bed before the scholar and his friend arrived.

Dinner was prepared by the time that an old but well-cared-for Daimler stopped in front of a mauve clematis that all but covered the entrance to the tower.

Once indoors, both visitors sighed in relief. Archibald Thorne acknowledged, silently and for the thousandth time, that Lettice for all her foolishness was more tolerable to be with than to think about – or, indeed, to correspond with. She flattered and fussed and turned her face up to show reverence.

Harold, the young professor, went to The Old Keep because he liked to be there and was uncritical of his hostess. From the start Archie had insisted on taking him along. She was kind to him, made him welcome and always introduced him, breathlessly, as Archie's 'colleague'.

It was good to be in a warm room after a quarrelsome journey.

'Now,' said Archibald, 'we want to meet Victoria.'

He was short and stocky.

'It's too disappointing. Poor darling isn't well. She's gone to bed. She was so hoping to talk to you about something of yours that she had just read.'

Archibald peered over his spectacles – an emphasised act.

'Some other time. Some other time. Nothing to worry about, I hope.'

'No. We're sure not. Overtired poor pet. Young marrieds have such a lot to cope with these days.'

Harold, unnerved by the mention of anything as intimate as female indisposition, stared at the fire and wondered how to speak. Later, next week, he would write to Lettice and tell her how wonderful it had been and how sorry he was not to have met Victoria.

Edgar went upstairs and Lettice said, 'I can't tell you how thrilled we both are with Victoria. She's unsophisticated but highly intelligent. That job she had in Italy says a lot. You would have loved talking to her but I fear we shall have to keep her in bed tomorrow.'

Archie Thorne relaxed. He had not particularly wanted to discuss his own works with a sensitive young lady.

Lettice's dog, a spaniel called Orpheus, slouched by a card table and Archie, a self-confessed and public loather of caninity in any form declared, not for the first time, 'As you know, I consider Orpheus to be almost as good as no dog at all. Almost, but not quite.'

With that he went upstairs and didn't come down until dinnertime when Lettice gave him a loud 'cooee'.

Chapter 2

They ate dinner in the rustic kitchen – all that remained of an ancient bake-house, adorned with ornamental gourds and specimen thistles.

'Archie, you have got to encourage Roland. He's got nerves about the exhibition. He even tells me that he won't have enough work finished in time. Have a little more *poison maison*.'

Archie had drained his glass and held it up in a manicured hand.

'Put it off. Put it off. Never work to a deadline. It destroys everything worth striving for. Your work is brilliant because of its precision, not because of dash and frenzy. Put it off.'

Harold looked down. Lettice had appealed to Archie and he had knowingly escaped her.

There had been deliberate cruelty in his advice and he went on in the same vein, speaking to Roland.

'What possible point can there be in your having a London exhibition? It has never come to my ears that you have difficulty selling your work. I only say this because I recognise your talent.'

Harold drew up his gangling legs and lodged his feet on the rung of a bentwood chair. He didn't understand why Archie was talking so wildly and upsetting Lettice, when he had been offered so little of the horrible wine. He realised that Archie found Roland and Lettice depressing since he was always contentious before going there and often silent on the way home.

Harold stayed there because of his involvement with Archie and wondered if he had ever known how Archie had become established as a regular guest – or even if Archie knew himself. He decided to ask him when they were in Wales.

Lettice gave news of her other children.

Bobby and Bobby had a daughter, also called Bobby. They were living in an artistic community somewhere in France. Lettice said that she thought the extended family was probably the best solution for nowadays.

Archie exploded. 'Commune! How can you allow it? Do you really mean to tell me that your son and daughter-in-law have joined a group personified by types with straggling locks, bushy beards and bare feet? Do they believe that they stand for the primitive man and the early Christian – Robinson Crusoe and Jesus Christ – the noble savage, wild men of the woods and the prophet whose kingdom is not of this world? Really Lettice. I'm ashamed of you both.' His words were pistol shots blasting sacred air. Lettice, straining to smile, cried, 'Archie. I've always maintained that you were an *enfant terrible*.'

Harold thought about it at length before he went to sleep.

In the morning, Archie was strutting round Harold's bed-room.

'Do you think that Victoria is being deliberately suppressed?'

Black spirals of hair fell over Harold's thin face. Brushing them back with a bony hand, he considered the question.

'No. Oh no. I'm sure not. What an idea. Why should they? She sounds rather wonderful.'

'Voices came from their room just now. I simply wondered. But no. Of course. You are right. It was perfectly frightful of me.'

Harold was alert. 'Archie. Don't be bad. It makes me desperate.'

At breakfast they were pressed to honey from the comb, as Lettice, got up to the nines for church, told them, 'Victoria is a little better. I have tried to persuade her to stay in bed but she insists on coming down for luncheon. Do remember, both of you, not to expect to see her at her best. If she talks too much it's just shyness and if she doesn't talk at all then it's shyness, too. Please be kind.'

Everybody went to church except Harold who wanted to walk in the woods and Victoria who had not left her room.

Before the church party returned, Harold, waxy-faced and slightly toothy, went into the sitting room – a bow-windowed extension to the tower added at a later date. He sat silently in a rank dark suit and watched Victoria closely as she huddled by the fireplace obscured by green knitting and cigarette smoke. She had tried harder than usual with her appearance and the effort had made her uneasy. Her brown hair was curly and prettily brushed but despite her tidiness it seemed that a small disturbance might blow the whole thing into confusion.

The others came in, superficially chastened by the church service.

Lettice, barely hiding disapproval at the sight of knitting and leaning backwards to avoid cigarette smoke, dug her fingers into Victoria's arm.

'Now, darling. I want you to meet one of our oldest friends. Archibald Thorne. I can see that you and Harold have already made friends. Whatever you do, don't let Archie bully you. He can be an absolute beast.'

Archie saw humour in the girl's face, which surprised him. He went forward to charm her.

'Is that a jumper for Edgar? Aren't you girls wonderful! Not only do you pledge yourselves to these young men for life but you knit jumpers for them as well. Lettice. Did you ever knit a jumper for Roland?'

Victoria laughed. She said that she was having a hippy phase and was knitting herself a poncho-cum-trouser suit, but planned to make a jumper for Edgar as soon the present task was finished. He advanced further towards her, scowling and wagging a meaty hand. 'A poncho-cum-trouser suit! I suppose that you approve of the adolescent of today. The shock-headed and dishevelled, with hair that seems to have run to seed hiding neck and ears in whiskery overgrowth, make me sick. I've seen them. Believe me. They're everywhere, clad in patched jeans and dirty anoraks, padding hand in hand, sometimes with bare feet, along the city pavements. Horrible specimens of humanity.'

Victoria began to laugh. She liked him very much. He was

amused by her laughter and held up his hand in mock fear of her disapproval.

Then he advanced even closer wearing a slightly dragging, floppy suit. His shoes were rather bulgy but expensive look-ing. 'Have you ever heard of a pop group called the Rolling Stones?' The word 'pop' exploded as a Chinese firework. 'The leader of this repulsive group – I forget his name – referred to the Mona Lisa as a load of crap! A load of crap. There.' His eyes glittered above bifocals. Lettice trembled and feigned amused collusion with his whims, her face clouded by a desperate effort to appear affectionate and understanding. Archie con-tinued to address Victoria.

'My dear. You don't take me seriously, do you?'

'I don't know how to take you. You attack in areas where I hold no views.'

'No views! Do you mean to tell me that you hold no views on the hirsute and the hispid?' Onlookers were silent.

Edgar took Victoria's hand as if to protect her from further harassment.

Archie's chuckle and Victoria's obvious enjoyment made Lettice shudder but she ran for her camera and held her hand up in an urgent fashion. 'Never allow a golden moment to go unrecorded. Flashing smiles, please. Where's Orpheus? Dog-gy's included. Say it after me. Papa, potatoes, poultry, prunes and prisms. Say the words and your mouths will be set fair for the photograph.'

Harold strove to do her bidding but got no further than 'potatoes'.

Chapter 3

In the afternoon, Archie and Harold left in the Daimler. Harold was too nervous to have learned to drive. He manoeuvred his long legs into the space in front of the passenger seat.

Edgar and Victoria left too and, once back in London, he assured her that they would not return to The Old Keep until she was quite well.

'But you must understand Mother. She has a deadly time in the country with Father painting and listening to birdcalls on the gramophone. You resist the idea of giving in to her whims. It would be easier if you could accept her absurdities.'

'Does Archie Thorne really like her? How can he go there if he doesn't have to? Do you think it's to please Harold? Harold is too susceptible to wounds himself to censure others. I daresay he doesn't know many people to compare her with.'

'Archie started coming years ago. Somebody once told me that it was because of us when we were young. Archie's imagination has always been aroused by children – particularly boys. Not much interested in my sisters, if I remember right. When my brother and I were small he used to worry Papa by grunting and following us about on all fours. We didn't much mind but Papa once accused him of slavering and ordered him to stand up. Created a bit of an atmosphere at the time. Mama always insisted that it filled her with delight to see the generations interact. He's a bit of a rascal. Not quite a rogue. A rascal. He weighs in heavily on all the wrong sides. My parents have never known if he does it for effect or from conviction. I find it very tedious.' Edgar told her all this, clearing his throat, as though unmoved and uninterested.

'Do you think I might be having a baby?' Victoria asked.

'Of course you could be. Please, though, don't hope for it to be a boy in order to captivate Archie Thorne.

Chapter 4

Archie Thorne was in Piccadilly carrying a bowler hat and a trim umbrella when he saw Victoria. Wary in traffic, he looked about him before stepping across the road.

'Have you finished the poncho-cum-trouser suit?'

His trousers were short, stopping an inch above his laced shoes.

'I did finish it but it wasn't a huge success. It didn't fit properly. When I'd finished it I knitted a jumper for Edgar.'

'And he wears it all the time?'

'Not really. I think it's disappeared.'

'How perfectly frightful. Should we go into the Ritz and take a drink?'

On a curved sofa on the elevated area of the hall of the Ritz Hotel, they drank champagne. Archie asked her if she had recovered her strength.

'Both Harold and I were disappointed to have seen so little of you. I shall insist that we are all invited together another time.'

'Do you go there often?'

'Do we go there often? The answer is yes. I think I can say that we go regularly. Harold loves it. Lettice has been very kind to him.'

'I don't imagine that it would be difficult to be kind to Harold.'

'How about you? I can imagine that it might be difficult to marry a member of such a large and united family. Perhaps overpowering to start with?'

Again his spectacles were lowered and he looked at her with amusement. The lowering of spectacles reminded her of Laurence and she realised that it was time she wrote to him.

Victoria said, 'Lettice finds it more challenging to be nice to me than she does to Harold. It's difficult to fit into her picture. My clothes are no good. Perhaps it will come right.'

She touched his hand. 'I'm going to have a baby. Not for months and months, of course. I hope you don't mind my mentioning it.'

'Mind! There are a great many things that I do mind and this is not one of them. My dearest child. If we were not at the Ritz, which we are, I would put my arms round you and hug you. I should hug you.'

'I haven't told Lettice yet.'

'You must. You must let her know at once. Shall we send her a joint postcard?'

Chapter 5

The exhibition was only two weeks away. Roland never returned to the subject of postponing it and spent nearly all his time in the garden. The guest list was taking shape. The problems had become more complicated since Lettice had decided to give a small dinner party for intimate friends at the Ritz Hotel after the show.

She was not sure what to say to Victoria about this.

She rehearsed. 'Darling, I refuse to let you tire yourself just for a silly dinner. It would be different if Edgar could have been there to look after you.' Edgar had to be abroad on his printing-ink round. Victoria was certain to smoke between courses. Also, there had been that puzzling moment with Archie Thorne; something conspiratorial that spooked her. A complicity. He was expected to come to the dinner party and she did not wish to hear a repeat of their shared laughter.

A timid neighbour called to her from the window. Belinda, shrinking as she always did from self-assertion, had left her car on the road outside the garden boundary. She was the pretty daughter of an East Anglian rural dean and had been trained to believe in humility – a training from which she sometimes reared to relieve herself. That afternoon she wanted to take a cutting from one of Lettice's roses. Lettice, much pleased, said, 'How lovely for me to picture a bloom from my canary bird in your ravishing little garden. Nowhere could it fall on happier ground. To me canary bird is the symbol of summer and sunshine.'

When the cutting had been taken, although neither woman had the faintest idea if the time of year was right, Lettice invited Belinda to come indoors. She needed advice about the London dinner party.

Picking up a preliminary list, roughly written (bold italics kept for best), she waved at an armchair.

'I really don't know if I'm coming or going. The whole thing is a complete nightmare. So many people will be hurt. What can one do? I know that you and Jack will understand perfectly. We see so much of you down here that there's hardly any point in meeting in the beastly hurly-burly of London. Are our less sophisticated neighbours going to see it in the same sensible way? You can help me here. If we don't ask you (and you are known to be our closest country friends) then the others will be sure to accept it. What do you think?'

Belinda, aghast at being excluded, was too baffled and furious to answer.

Lettice's words came breathlessly.

'I can see that you, darling, agree with me entirely. I am

going to give a cosy little dinner party here as soon as we get back from London. You and Jack will be guests of honour and I promise to remember every ridiculous detail of the evening to amuse you all.'

Chapter 6

Victoria opened her letters. One was from Laurence. It gave her a turn to see her new name and address written in squared-off letters on an envelope with Italian stamps on it and written in Mungo Craddock's hand. Dictated by Laurence.

'My dear Victoria. I was overjoyed to hear the news that you are to become a mother. Not something you will do twenty-four times, I imagine. You are much missed here but I am very well looked after by Mungo.'

She pictured Mungo sitting, oiling up, prosy and pompous, beard twisted in watch chain.

'He has promised to stay with me for ever. We would welcome a visit from you at any time. Elena has been giving trouble by regularly handing in her notice. She cries, poor dear, and nobody can get to the bottom of it. Perhaps you will drop her a line?'

Victoria had never seen Archie Thorne's writing but had no doubt as to who the second letter came from. Black ink swirled over a thick envelope. She saved it up – dealing first with Laurence's and writing to Elena.

'My dear Victoria,' Archie started, 'Harold and I are going to Roland's exhibition. I write to say that I very much hope – and expect – to see you there. Lettice is giving a supper party afterwards at the Ritz – a place you are familiar with, no doubt. This is simply to say how much I hope to be placed next to you there. In great haste. Much love. Archie.'

A third letter was from Lettice.

'Darling. Oh! How beastly it must be for you. I remember it all so well. Do believe me when I tell you that it doesn't last for ever. And oh! What a miracle to look forward to! Now. Prepare yourself! I am going to be rather bossy! After the exhibition Roland and I are giving a tiny duty dinner party at the Ritz Hotel. I am simply determined that you should go home beforehand – especially since dear Edgar has to be abroad. I know he would never forgive me if I allowed you to tire yourself just for that. Please don't argue. I know that we try to please each other. This is why I speak bluntly. No nonsense now! All my love and thoughts go out to you at this exciting moment in your young life. Your devoted mother-in-law. Lettice.'

Victoria forwarded Lettice's letter to Archie. Then she wrote to Lettice saying that she would not dream of deserting her or Roland on this important occasion and that they could count on her presence at the Ritz.

Before he left for his business trip, she spoke to Edgar of her meeting with Archie in Piccadilly.

'You are lucky to have known him all your life. I wish he was my uncle or godfather or something with a label. I will never expect to be anything as exalted as his friend.'

'Why not? We could ask him here any time. I suppose my mother might be disconcerted.'

Lettice was certainly disconcerted when Victoria's letter arrived. She now thoroughly mistrusted her. Sweeping through the dusty drawing room to a corner where the daffodil telephone lived surrounded by chaotic papers on her desk, she dialled Belinda's number.

'I long to know if you've heard how the Grants and the Woolies have taken it. I dread hurting their feelings and I'm counting on you and Jack to smooth it all over for me.'

Belinda's vexation had festered and, encouraged by her husband, she had done all in her power to incite the fury of the other slighted neighbours.

'Another thing, Belinda, and I wouldn't say this to anyone but you, but I am in the most awful dilemma about Victoria. Being family, she assumes that she is included in the little dinner after the opening. I wrote to tell her that she must on no account come. I am worried that she might tire herself. Now she replies that she wouldn't dream of missing it. What am I to do next?'

'I'm sorry. I'm being silly but I don't understand the problem.'

'I can't have explained it properly. Everything is so frantic with such a short time to go. The problem is simple. What can I do about preventing Victoria from coming to the dinner?'

'Why do you want to prevent her?'

'Apart from her health – which is, of course, the main reason, I have to admit (but again to no one but you) that perhaps I am just a tiny bit protective about her in other ways. She is such a pet and I think it would be cruel to throw her in at the deep end quite so soon. I couldn't bear to see her humiliated beside so many intellectuals – for Edgar's sake as much as for her own.'

Belinda offered no advice and her voice faded on a less humble note than was usual.

Chapter 7

Lettice wrote to Victoria again.

'Darling. I cannot tell you how touched I was by your adorable letter. Families are such wonderful things. Nothing will ever replace them and Roland and I are so grateful to learn how strongly you want to become one of ours. I was determined from the start that you should not be overstrained by the exhibition and I made up my mind – long before your darling letter came. In fact, so determined was I that I had already made up a party of ten. You know the hatefulness of our financial position. Ten is the very maximum we can afford so there must be no more of your sweet selflessness. All my love and gratitude. I can't wait for this dreadful business to be over so that I can concentrate on your darling babe.'

In his college lodgings, Archie Thorne perused his mail. He put two letters to one side after reading those from the larger pile, sent for his secretary and asked her to deal with them.

Victoria's letter said, 'It is now certain that I won't be sitting next to you at the Ritz. Lettice is convinced that it would be bad for my health. It seems that it will do me no harm, however, to go to the crowded cocktail party beforehand so perhaps I'll see you there? Much love. Victoria.'

Lettice's letter was short.

'Dearest Archie. The great day draws near! It is sweet of you and Harold to say that you will come and support us at the Ritz dinner. The table is booked for eight thirty sharp so don't dally at the party. How I wish it were all over! What one will do for art's sake! Fondest love. Lettice.'

Archie slid both letters across the mahogany table. Harold read them with an expression of pain.

'Oh dear. It is certainly unfortunate. But, then, it is hard to put oneself into either position.'

Victoria could not squeeze into anything suitable. A friend arrived with a choice of loose frocks. They picked out a mauve one with a low-cut neckline.

The friend said, 'Let's buy mauve stockings and shoes. You'll look terrific.'

After locking her car, Victoria ran along the street towards the gallery. Her dread of the gathering was great and she was urged forward by nervous courage. Stopping for a while on the pavement, she peeped in through the window. Inside, at the foot of a staircase, there was a table covered by a white cloth. The staircase led to an upper level and a white-coated man stood behind the table handing out glasses as a grim group walked past her and turned into the gallery. One after another they stopped at a small table just inside the door to sign their names in a visitor's book. A record of the great event. Something for Lettice's memoirs. Victoria followed them but didn't add her name.

Before she secured a drink, Lettice caught sight of her. They kissed. Two figures dressed in mauve.

'Darling. It's too extraordinary. It shows what a great affinity we must have. Robert. Come and meet my daughter-in-law.'

The painter beamed. 'But she's one of my favourite girls. Jolly good at watercolours, too. Roland must be pleased about that.'

Lettice knew nothing of Victoria and watercolours but managed a smile through taut lips.

Robert Stratton had stayed once, and only for a night or two, with Laurence at the villa on his way to Rome. He had encouraged her as she sketched on the terrace.

Happy to find a sympathiser there, Victoria asked him when he had arrived in London.

Lettice, as exotically got up as she had planned to be, silenced her.

'Now, dearest. I am going to talk to Robert. I haven't seen him for months and living, as I do, under a curtain of moss and ivy, probably won't see him for months to come.'

There was a whirl in Victoria's head. She stepped back and it came to her that she was not only obscuring a picture of a thrush but possibly damaging it as well. She turned round and examined it. It was an unusual example of Roland's work since it included a human figure. On her first visit to The Keep he had asked her if she would sit for him. She had sat for many hours under a cedar tree. The thrush had flown away. He had been painted in advance. Now she remembered how peaceful it had been and how stirred she had been by the attention. Maybe she only liked old men. The painting did not seem, to her, to be a very good one. The hands were badly drawn and the eyelashes odd; straight rows of twigs.

Archie was suddenly beside her. 'I see that you came to the exhibition to look at one painting only!'

'No. It was a mistake. I didn't know what to do and fell at the nearest point.'

'I hope you don't expect me to understand a word of what you are saying. Shall I fetch you a drink?'

Archie had intended to return but was waylaid by a male member of the group that Victoria had followed in to the party. Now that she saw his face, she recognised it as belonging to a man of fame in the world of art. She was not surprised to see how obviously Archie was enjoying the encounter, nor was she perplexed at being so quickly forgotten.

She would like to have talked to Harold who was standing, mute, close by but decided not to. They would only look at each other as they had done on that Sunday morning at The Old Keep. His closeness to Archie puzzled and hypnotised her.

Lettice was near; clasping the hand of one of her daughters, a plain girl of nineteen. She drew her towards a smartly dressed young man.

'I don't believe you two have ever met.'

They stood face to face until Lettice's eyes were fixed elsewhere.

Archie collected them together. Lettice, Victoria and Harold.

'Lettice. This is a wonderful party. I am delighted to see Victoria again and especially pleased to see her so well. She is such a new acquisition for your family that I fear it would be presumptuous of me to ask if I might be placed next to her at dinner.'

Harold turned away as Lettice bridled.

'Hasn't Archie got an uncanny instinct for learning one's secrets? Victoria, you mustn't be cross with me. I shall have to tell Archie the reason why you have decided to go straight home to bed after the party.' Brushing his face with a part of her head gear, Lettice whispered news into Archie's ear.

Victoria went to where Harold stood.

'I think I could hate Archie.'

'Yes. Oh dear yes. I understand – but he would never do anything bad enough to make you hate him. I have a great deal of experience to draw on and I know that he would never do anything bad enough for that.'

She stayed by Harold until the party started to disband.

Archie suggested that they sit down together for a few minutes on the step of the staircase that led to the upper gallery.

'You ought not to have been angry with me. I was teasing Lettice. It doesn't do her any harm. I don't believe she even notices.'

'You were teasing me, too – and Harold.'

'Was I?'

Guests walked past them and out into the street.

When eleven people remained, Lettice went to the step.

'Archie. We must make haste to the Ritz.' She wasn't sure if he listened to her.

'Did you hear me? We must go to the Ritz. It's getting late.'

Archie and Victoria were planning a future meeting.

'You shall come and stay with me in Cambridge. Harold and I will show you the sights.'

What was to be seen of Lettice's parchment face from under her floppy, flowered hat, was strained and angry. On the verge of blasphemy, she cried, 'Archie. You must come to the Ritz now whether you like it or not.'

Chapter 8

Roland and Lettice, Archie and Harold, Alice (the nine-teen-year-old daughter), the prosperous young man, the celebrated figure from the world of art and his inebriated wife, a minor poet and a famous composer of quartets walked, one behind the other, into the magnificent dining room at the Ritz Hotel.

Archie sat between the minor poet and the teenage daughter.

Lettice warbled, 'It's awful how I always seem to know more men than women.' She explained to the composer of quartets, 'I'm afraid I find men more interesting. Although I say it, I have never been a one to suffer fools gladly.'

Then, straining every muscle of her face, she turned to the famous fellow from the world of art who was placed on her right. She had rubbed up on her knowledge of the offerings of cultural London that morning as her hair was being twisted into coils. Her chirpy hairdresser took an interest in art and had given her some tips.

'I gather there's a new print of *Le Jour Célèbre* at the Academy.'

Roland, sharp of hearing, called across, '*Le Jour Se Lève*, Lettice. I imagine that's what you are talking about.'

Her daughter, talking to Archie, asked, 'Are you interested in psychoanalysis? I think it's fascinating. Honestly, you wouldn't believe how many problems stem from having been misunderstood as a child.'

Roland, on her other side, said, 'I hope none of you are going to start believing that you were misunderstood.'

Months of Lettice's plotting had led to this occasion.

Alice went on. 'Freud was fantastic. Did you know that it was him who said, "There's no such thing as bad weather, only the wrong clothes". Don't you think that's fantastic?'

Archie was wondering if Victoria was safely back at home. He planned to ring her after dinner.

Harold's energy had dribbled away and he could barely lift his food to his mouth. When dinner was over he thanked Lettice, congratulated Roland and ran away.

Archie saw his lanky figure as he scrambled into a taxi. Dismissing the idea of trying to follow him, he decided that he would definitely ring Victoria. After all he would see Harold the next day when they dined in college hall.

Back at the flat, Victoria's mood was unsatisfactory. Her dislike of Lettice was uncomfortable. She wished that she missed Edgar. She had fallen asleep and had been dreaming again. Her baby, a boy, had blue eyes and grey curls. The telephone rang.

'I wanted to be sure that you got home all right.'

'How was dinner at the Ritz?'

'Very nice. It would have been a great deal nicer if you had been present.'

'Who did you sit next to?'

'Your sister-in-law. Very sweet. She talks about Freud and Jung.'

'Come and tell me about it.'

'Very well.'

He appeared on her doorstep almost instantly. He drank whisky and talked entertainingly of his rage at the abolition of capital punishment, dislike of facial hair, terror of men who wore earrings and his loathing of dogs which, he declared, ought to be muzzled at both ends. But he was tired and didn't stay as long as Victoria would have wished. His lunatic attitude was compelling and spellbinding. His jokes and his rages; his bigoted views and flirtatious manners lifted Victoria's spirits. She had never heard anything like it and compared him, neither favourably nor the opposite, with Laurence and his gentle liberal ways.

In days to follow she was uneasy. She was fearful of having been impertinent, notwithstanding the fact that he had telephoned her, in asking Archie to visit her after the Ritz dinner party. She wished that he didn't occupy such a distinguished position. Perhaps, when he retired, she would be allowed to visit him once a week.

Another Italian stamp and Mungo's exasperating handwriting on the hall floor at breakfast time. She was pleased though to hear from Laurence.

Less so when she discovered that the letter had not been dictated but came from Mungo Craddock himself.

'Dear Victoria. One writes to put you in the picture. Laurence is fading fast, poor old dear. He doesn't leave his bedroom and Aldo (do you recall the male nurse?) is on permanent standby.'

Did she recall the male nurse? Barely – and Laurence's routine had constituted her life for a while.

'Fear not! He wants for nothing. One reads aloud to him during his periods of consciousness; mostly from one's own works. One's style delights him. One has moved into the sitting room which, you may remember, is next to his bedroom. This way one can be on tap around the clock. Don't put yourself to the inconvenience of writing. He remembers nothing. Elena has let him down badly. One never took to her, truth be told. Her eyes are odd. One noticed them on one's first arrival at the villa. Do you recollect the occasion?'

A pitiful note came from Elena by the same post. It was not easy to decipher but told that she was powerless. The *buffo* had taken over. He flattered the cook and shunned her, Elena, mocking poor Dante and his gifts for the *padrone*; treasures from the shore. Sea horses and shells.

Bernadini had been summoned and it was rumoured that the *buffo* was involved with the redrafting of a will. She, Elena, had never expected anything but what did the *signorina* imagine? Perhaps the right to live with Dante in one of the outlying buildings. She had worked there since she was thirteen – and now she was thirty and ready to settle. Another thing. The *padrone* had been calling out for the *signorina*. Had the *buffo* told her this?

Chapter 9

Unsold paintings stacked in the hall reminded Lettice of her promise to Belinda. It was a week since the exhibition and Roland was out of humour.

Victoria sent a note to say that she had enjoyed the party and had also heard that the dinner had been a great success.

Who had she heard it from? It could only be Archie. 'Touch wood and whistle,' she told herself.

Shaken and emboldened by desire to investigate, Lettice decided to ask her to stay for a few days before Edgar returned from peddling ink in Yugoslavia.

'Darling. What a lovely letter! Roland and I both long to have you here and the country air would do you good. What about next week? Monday would suit perfectly. After all the people we had to fit in during our London visit, it is paradise to be alone and to listen to birdsong. The dawn chorus was unimaginable *ce matin*. I think Roland feels a little flat now it is all over and we rely on you to come and cheer us up. *Soignez-vous bien*. All fondest thoughts. Lettice.'

Victoria replied that, alas, she had been invited to stay in Cambridge for two nights that week. Archie, in his letter of invitation said, 'I want to see you very badly. I am not in a very good way generally and need a change. One that your presence would supply. My head and various parts of my body seem to lead separate existences so that I am watching myself and over-hearing myself the whole time, and not only my memory but my power of connected thinking seem to be removed from each other; I feel like a department store suffering from a power cut and with alarm bells sounding in all parts of the building (little pricks and tingles in limbs and extremities) which I interpret as signals, not of fire or gas but of closing time. But I am getting morbid and writing to excite pity. It's not really as bad as that but I do feel low, partly because I want to see you and partly because Harold is rather (but not entirely) withdrawn and I feel somehow at a loss. Please come soon. Love Archie.'

Victoria, overwhelmed in joy at thus being minimally con-fided in, had accepted his invitation by return of post.

'Holy mackerel!' Lettice started to panic and to talk to her-self. 'Cambridge! How had she heard that the dinner party went well? It can't be Archie and Harold, can it? I don't see how. What am I to do – buried here among the mossy banks?'

Chapter 10

Victoria drove to Cambridge. She was greeted at the door of the leaden-looking lodgings by a polite college servant who told her that the principal awaited her upstairs in his study. As Victoria, heavily pregnant, walked quietly into the room, Archie Thorne rose from his chair and lowered his spectacles. It was unnerving to see him there. Principal of a college.

'I am terribly pleased to see you.'

Victoria inspected the room – donnish with piled pieces of paper spilling over each other. She was taken aback to see, among other works of art, so many indifferent portraits of young men – some with ruby lips and many unclad.

'So. You are admiring my paintings, I see. The one that I particularly like is the one on your right.' The picture on her right showed nothing but gravestones. 'Rather gloomy,' she said.

'I like it. It is named *Churchyard* and the best thing about it is that the artist himself is also called Churchyard. My colleague, Harold, who you know well, will join us at teatime. He is terribly excited to think that he is going to see you again very soon. He was so excited last evening that he brought a tea tray down on my head.' Archie put his hand to his temple, winced and said, 'It was frightfully thrilling but fortunate that none of the fellows of the college were about.'

She joined Archie in the study where a tea tray had appeared. She wondered if it was the one to have been brought down on Archie's head by Harold in his excited anticipation of seeing her again.

'Ah. Here comes Harold. Harold. I have been telling Victoria how you have been looking forward to her visit.'

'No. No. You mustn't.'

'Mustn't what?'

'Say anything.'

Harold then fell silent and remained so until he left with no warning and looking haunted.

Victoria asked Archie if everything was in order. 'Of course. He's dreadfully sensitive, you know. I think, another time, you would do well to admire his looks. As I often say, he is a plant that needs watering every day.'

'Did I not water enough then? I tried to hug him when he arrived but he shied away.'

'My child. You did nothing wrong whatsoever. He was overcome with pleasure. Now. Tell me how things are. How is your mother-in-law?'

An enticing and seductive evening passed, Archie's firebrand conversation occasionally interrupted by the wafting in and out of Harold. He never settled or joined them as they ate but was not violent or destructive at any stage. Archie gazed at him with tolerant adoration and some awe as he came and went.

Victoria was none the wiser and was glad that she had only arranged to stay for one night. The oddity of Harold's behaviour had been, at times, hard to handle.

Part Three

Chapter 1

Edgar returned from his ink round feeling unwell. He took to his bed and complained that it was nothing worse than a weakness in the limbs but, within days, he was taken to hospital having moaned and turned a yellowish colour in the middle of one night. Victoria sent him away in an ambulance for she was due to give birth at any time. Before arranging her own transport to the hospital, she rang Lettice.

'You poor pet.' Her mother-in-law, roused from sleep, managed to sound alive. 'What an added worry at this traumatic time. It must be the catching type of jaundice, since darling Edgar, as you know, has never been tempted by excess. *Grâce à Dieu.*'

At the hospital a nurse said that Edgar was suffering from something called an enlarged heart. Strange, Victoria thought, that he should suffer physically from a complaint never to have affected him in the emotional sense.

As he died, Victoria was lifted onto a truckle bed and

trundled to the delivery room. Edgar drew his last breath as his daughter, Maudie, took her first.

Victoria had never been as happy.

Lettice, distraught, ran along the corridor from the cubicle where she had kissed the corpse, to the Maternity Wing where she kissed, with equal fervour, the corpse's widow and child.

Edgar's sister, Alice, peeped in. 'You poor thing. It's awful to talk like this but I feel I must explain something. The first day in a baby's life is by far the most important in its development. They pick up waves of sorrow. It sounds silly to people who haven't studied my subject but I promise you, and I am in my second year, you must try to forget what is happening down the passage and concentrate like mad on the poor little baby.'

Victoria beamed and Alice spread the news of her courage.

She stayed in hospital for a week – missing Edgar's funeral.

Chapter 2

Lettice photographed the coffin from every angle squinting into the top of a square Rolex camera. At a cold lunch at The Old Keep following the funeral, she told Archie that she had taken to photography by accident; that a darling old friend had left the beloved Rolex behind after staying with her and had died before she had time to return it to him by post. 'I began at once and modelled myself on that fascinating woman who photographed our very own Alfred, Lord Tennyson on the Isle of Man.'

'Wight,' Archie said. 'Quite Wight.'

Later she compiled an album, which she gave to Victoria for her birthday. It included one picture of the coffin – close up and smothered in wild flowers and shrivelled ferns. Under it she had written the caption 'Edgar's coffin. Our flowers.'

The artistic son and his wife had hastened back from France for the funeral but were too distracted by their free-range child to concentrate on the purpose of their journey, and the community in France had wired to say that the system was collapsing without the three Bobbies so they departed immediately after the church service. Roland, numb and dumb, suffered noticeably. Lettice, snapping and flashing, looked wretchedly unhappy too, particularly when Archie told her that he intended to visit Victoria and Maudie.

'Archie, you are an angel.' Thus he felt free to go with a clear conscience.

Roland visited Victoria in hospital. He kissed the baby and left as soon as he dared.

Archie wrote, 'What can I say? I could write a good deal but would prefer to talk to you. Of course I would sooner you had given birth to a son but I will come and see you, if I may. Maudie is a pretty name and I'm sure you are already a wonderful mother. Your news has revived me and I no longer believe myself to be in a department store at closing time. Best love.'

Victoria answered, 'Dearest Archie. You are very kind. Please come but don't put yourself out. Don't come if you think it might bother Lettice. It is terrible for her. I do hope that you will though. Best love.'

Archie went to see her the day after the funeral.

During Archie's visit he told Victoria, 'Lettice knew of my coming and approved of my doing so.'

He did not ask to see the baby. She was in another room with a label on her wrist.

Victoria knew that, soon, there was to be no alternative but for her to go, indefinitely, to live at The Old Keep for she was short of money.

Amongst many letters Victoria received concerning her double event, a grizzly one came from Northern Italy.

Mungo had spotted both items in Laurence's airmail edition of the *Times* and wrote to say, 'Laurence would, most certainly, have bidden one to comment on your news both sad and glad. The poor old dear is slipping away fast. One has been efficacious in persuading him to receive the priest. Elena has proved herself to be the most frightful stumbling block and refused to show him up. As one mentioned before, one's first instincts were consistent with facts, she is a thorn in everyone's flesh. One can't think what's got into her. After all, peasants are surely of the faith.'

Poor Elena. How painful for her to witness the agnostic Laurence being got at. The *buffo* went on to say, 'It cannot be long now. Have no fear. The old dear is in excellent hands.'

A packet of sea horses came for Maudie. Elena had wrapped them carefully in a padded envelope and for the first time since widowhood, Victoria wept.

At The Old Keep Victoria and Maudie slept in a room at the top of the tower. Victoria had specially requested this. The winding stairs were tricky with a baby to carry up and down but it gave privacy. It was rum up there. At one stage there had been six openings in the brickwork, cutting through and randomly punctuating the thick wall. In these gaps doves had rested; billing and cooing. Lettice, never eager to tamper with the picturesque, had glassed them in – or rather glassed them out. Panes, flat against the inside wall, had been slotted into place. Sprig-muslin curtains cuddled round them like peek-a-boo bonnets, pinned permanently open, never destined to be drawn. Each tiny curtained window, air neither entering nor escaping, framed doves – comfortable each night in time-worn resting places.

Victoria lay awake, alert, as birds landed and left, teased and tumbled as though on six television sets but more enthralling. In one window a plump, ruffled and fluffed pair pecked at each other, beady-eyed.

In another three were squeezed in side by side, bored and sedentary. Archie and Harold in the first perhaps; then the three Bobbies.

Above Maudie's cot a third pair perched. They preened and praised. Lettice and Roland. Above this there was a small resting place where a solitary bird gazed and met her eyes. Antics varied from box to box and at one moment she saw a pale and hazy Edgar drift away without flurry. By morning every bird had flown.

Most of the neighbours knew that Lettice had her daughter-in-law and baby granddaughter staying with her.

Belinda was the first to call. Hoping that the tragedy had taken Lettice's mind off the sale of Roland's bird sketches, she sidled past the stack of frames propped against the entrance-hall wall – as they had been for many months.

Victoria pressed her cigarette into the heart of a rose and opened the parcel that Belinda handed to her. Out slid an exquisitely crocheted pink cardigan for Maudie.

Lettice wafted in and told Belinda that visiting hours were strict and that her time was up.

In the hall she asked Belinda to take the painting with her. 'Somehow you always seem to forget it. Don't bother about the cheque today. Any time will do as long as it's before those horrid statements come at the end of the month.'

Later, Lettice sorted through a pile of old photographs – mostly taken by herself. She told Victoria that the likeness between Maudie and Edgar was uncanny and that through Maudie Edgar lived on.

—— Chapter 3 ——

Early one morning Lettice came into Victoria's bedroom. 'Darling. I know this may seem old-fashioned to one of your generation but, when we have Maudie christened, I think you will feel a little something. I wonder who the godparents should be? I think Edgar would have liked us to ask Archie Thorne. I know he's old but he is a famous figure and it might be fun for Maudie to talk about him in years to come.'

Victoria put in a plea for Caroline; the friend who had lent her the mauve dress and persuaded her to buy mauve stockings before Roland's exhibition, but Lettice gave no sign of having heard her. When Lettice had left her alone with her baby, she wrote to Archie. 'Lettice thinks you should be Maudie's god-father. I don't know why. I'd imagined she was bothered by our having made friends in the first place. Please do though. I'd be thrilled.'

Downstairs and using a relief nib, Lettice wrote to Archie. 'Such a favour to ask! Would you be an angel and take on another godchild? I know you have dozens (including my Alice), but Victoria hasn't any idea as to how to go about things and, if we aren't firm, might neglect to have the mite "done" at all. Bless you. *A bientôt.* Lettice.'

Then she rang Belinda. 'Darling. A thousand thanks for the cheque. It is miserable that we couldn't make a special price for you but, with these poor bereft darlings to feed, the pinch is worse than ever. Thank God Victoria has seen sense and has bidden me ask Archie Thorne to be Maudie's godfather. Darling Archie is such a pet. I know he won't refuse and, being a bachelor… Did I tell you that he went to see them in hospital for me?'

Archie wrote, 'Dearest Victoria. Of course. Delighted to make vows for Maudie. Will I be able to keep them? Naturally, if she ever misbehaves I shall simply box her ears. Could you ask Harold to be a godfather as well? He needs to be included. Don't forget. He is a plant that has to be watered every day. Who can do this better than you?'

Then he wrote to Lettice. 'I am delighted to take on another godchild. All of mine are grown up. Isn't your daughter-in-law wonderful? In haste.'

Chapter 4

Maudie was christened in July. Both godfathers presented her with signed editions of their own published works. Archie's was on the life of some obscure scholar and Harold's on pure mathematics.

Lettice enthused, 'Fascinating for when she's older. I believe Archie gave the same one to Alice at her christening.'

Belinda and Jack walked back to their car after the tea party following the baptism and Jack said, 'It depends on what sort of thing little Maudie is going to find fascinating.'

Victoria ran after them and put in a plea.

'I wish I could come over to see you. Is there a bus?'

Belinda assured her that they were only a ten-minute walk away and promised to arrange something. 'When the godfathers are out of the way.'

Later she telephoned Lettice. 'You must be longing for a rest. Let me have Victoria and Maudie for a few nights. Jack cooks and hoovers all day and makes me feel redundant. I'd love to be of use.'

Lettice was exhausted from trying to keep up the delicate country house atmosphere for days on end and drove them to Belinda's as soon as decency allowed.

When she arrived at Jack and Belinda's cosy-looking farm-house Victoria steeled herself to face several facts. She had become attached to many new people and she had met them all through Lettice. She wouldn't have had Maudie if it hadn't been for Edgar and he, of course, had come through Lettice in a manner of speaking.

Jack and Belinda had one son. He had been born, unex-pectedly, after years of yearning. He was nine years old and coming to the end of his first year at boarding school. Belinda schemed endlessly for excuses to justify going to look at him. Regulated visiting hours set out by the school were worse than inadequate. He received more parcels than ever recorded in the institution's history – or at any rate in the memory of Miss Dancy, the neurotically fat matron who despised over-indul-gent mothers and challenged neglectful ones. Belinda used to wait impatiently for Arthur's demanding letters. Whilst Jack cooked and hoovered she would crouch on the floor mak-ing up neat packets of new pencils, chocolates and stamps as Lettice, at The Old Keep, repeatedly insisted to Roland, 'Poor Arthur. It's a crime to have only one child.'

Victoria adored staying with Belinda. Maudie slept in the garden in a pram once lain in by Arthur, for hours at a time, as Victoria sat by the fire on the stained and splitting leather of a club fender, smoking and knitting as she watched Belinda, another knitter, turn the heel of a sock for Arthur or, with a mouthful of pins, stitch at a curtain for his bedroom window.

Finding it as hard to remember Edgar as many find it hard to forget a figure whose death has altered the course of life, Victoria was unable to concentrate on the query of her future.

That it was not to be as it might have been was a realisation vast enough.

Belinda said, 'I'd like to keep you here for ever.'

Victoria pictured the trouble that Lettice would have in accepting or even allowing such a situation to exist at the same time as hailing it. A way might be found.

'Obviously not for ever. Simply for the period necessary for the finding of a solution.'

Victoria was untroubled by thoughts that she and Maudie could be burdens on Belinda or Jack, who had developed a tenderness towards Maudie. His capacity for tenderness had lain untapped since Arthur had slumbered in the same pram.

Lettice rang Belinda.

'Darling. Are you alone? I hope it isn't too exhausting for you. I know what it is to have a treasured mite in the house. Drop a hint and I'll be over to fetch them back.'

Belinda, in quiet agreement, allowed Lettice to confer favours.

'If it really is a help, and I know how lonely you are, I will admit that I do need a little longer on my own – with Roland and my beloved books – to recover from shock and sadness.'

It had been arranged and Victoria and Maudie stayed on.

There was no money – or not enough.

Edgar had not taken out an insurance policy on his life.

There was the furniture, some wedding presents and a small sum left to Victoria by her mother. Her father, it seemed to her, had always been dead.

Jack and Belinda drew close.

One of them, it was never known which, thought of the stables. It had always been a possibility that one day they would prop them up; improve the value of the property – an increased legacy for Arthur. They made an inspection. There were damp patches and dry rot but structurally the building was sound. It could be done. Jack and local builders set to work and in less than four months the place was inhabitable.

Victoria and Maudie moved in and Lettice breathed freely.

'Of course Belinda is a saint. There's nothing she wouldn't do for me. To have Victoria and the precious baby nearby and yet not close enough to be a daily reminder of the loss of darling Edgar, is all I could have dreamed of. Naturally we would have found a solution but Belinda needs a companion – so few friends – and I'd hate to deprive her.'

Chapter 5

Laurence expired. The news was broken to Victoria in two ways. One by letter from Mungo and another, tear-drenched, from Elena.

The first, 'One is proud to tell you that Laurence died serenely having rejoiced in the benefit of last rites. Father Sorbi took it into account that the old dear had never been received into the church. His peace of mind, at the end, was most rewarding. Rewarding and rousing. One hopes soon, when things are sorted out, to be in a position to offer you some little memento, a keepsake in memory of your time here.'

Elena wrote, '*Signorina*. Tragedy. The *padrone* is dead. Dead, *Signorina*.'

Elena had not been allowed to see him – had not been allowed near him – and had the *padrone* not always counted on her? She had been his eyes. Her slit ones had seen for him. Did the *signorina* remember the day when she found the clock? The alarm clock lost in a drawer? She, Elena, had set it ticking in the nick of time.

Links with Italy were over. Gone. Printer's ink. Edgar and Puccini. Even Archie seemed to have evaporated. He seemed to neglect or to forget her.

A longed-for letter came early in December. It was wrapped around a small Battersea box that he sent as a Christmas present for Maudie.

'Dearest Victoria,' he wrote. 'Will you please forgive me for (apparent) ingratitude and neglect and lack of affection and good manners and all that makes life worth living? I have been tired and distracted, unable to concentrate on work. Here I have sat, day after day, immersed (almost literally immersed because the college is closed). I am just working and working. Not hard work – just intellectual knitting. You know a lot about knitting. Checking texts, revising punctuation, filling in blanks, confirming proper names, etc. No real thinking. I drop stitches purposely now and again, just to postpone the end and to defer the need for thought or creative writing. I haven't written a letter for nearly a fortnight. I've often said to myself, "I'll write a letter to Victoria when I've finished the next row..." – my metaphor for knitting. That metaphor makes me think of you. Now the vacation has started and I hope to see you. I hear from Lettice of your arrangement with neighbours. I hope that it is all that it should be. Might I come and see for myself? Lettice has invited us both (Harold and me) to spend the New Year at The Keep so, doubtless, we will see you then. What would be even better, however, would be to meet beforehand. Let me know if you are able to think of a plan.

'PS. I hope that Maudie is good and well.' The word 'good' was underlined four times.

Lettice, hacking in the cabbage patch, counted her disappointments. Edgar was dead. The Bobbies communed in France. Alice was a dear, Roland's favourite, but would always be plain. Joanna, still a schoolgirl and soon to come home for the Christmas holidays, seemed to be part of another world. It was unlikely that they would ever hear from Maurice again. He had gone to America six years earlier and had become a Mormon – or was it a Jehovah's Witness? Perhaps a Shaker? Whatever the group he had joined, it precluded him from further communication with his family or with connections to life before his conversion.

Lettice had tried a heart-rending letter when Edgar died but had not had a reply. When making final vows Maurice had been permitted to write once to his mother stating the facts but not giving the reasons for his compulsory farewell.

Horrible fears formed in her head.

Had she been unwise in allowing Victoria to escape? Archie Thorne liked her. She had to absorb that fact and abandon hope that the vague but apparent conspiracy sprang from loyalty to herself. Then there had been Robert at Roland's exhibition. 'Know her? She's one of my favourite girls.'

Watercolour paintings? She had seen no sign of such a talent. A rival to Roland? 'Holy mackerel.'

Were the stables, Belinda and Jack's stables, going to threaten her supremacy? Two loose boxes had become two spare bedrooms. Archie and Harold? Heaven knew who else?

Belinda in the centre of it all – fawning but triumphant. Had Belinda seen chances?

She rang her.

'Dearest. Our sorrow will be with us always but thanks to your kindness in caring for Victoria and Maudie when we were plunged into a wilderness of despair, we are coming to terms with it. It's forever ahead, I know, but I want to book you in for New Year's Eve. I'll be over in a day or two – a little nonsense for Maudie. *A tout à l'heure.*'

Victoria answered Archie's letter.

'Do come and bring Harold. You can both stay with me. Everything is wonderful. If you don't come and see for yourself (as you suggest you might) but rely on my description, you might simply think I was being brave. Thank you for asking about Maudie and for the ravishing box. I have put it away carefully and will show it to her on Christmas Day. You ask if she is good. She is perfect. Almost too good and doesn't interrupt nearly often enough. You must see her for yourself for, again, if you relied on my description you would simply think that I was boasting. Please come for a night or two – or more – before Christmas and don't worry about Lettice. Belinda will find a way round the trickiness.'

Remembering the plant in need of constant watering, she wrote to Harold as well. She said how much she hoped to see him installed in one of her loose boxes before long.

Chapter 6

Archie and Harold walked slowly along The Parade. They often did this in the early afternoon. Harold leaned towards Archie, bending to catch his words.

'I don't see why we shouldn't go and stay with Victoria for a few days before Christmas. After all, we go to Lettice for the New Year.'

Harold, unwilling to allow that Lettice had failings, did not accept that their decision might affect her. It was a question of whether they wanted to go.

'I think it would be pleasant. Very pleasant indeed.'

'Very well. I shall write to Victoria and propose that we go for two nights next week.'

'Dearest Victoria. So. We come to see for ourselves. We will be with you, short of any serious accident on the road, at tea-time next Wednesday. Until then.'

Belinda tried to be wise. 'As long as Lettice can persuade herself that they only come to see you for her sake I think you'll get away with it.'

Victoria wrote a note.

'Dear Lettice. Archie and Harold have decided to take their godparental duties seriously so they are coming here for two nights next week, Wednesday and Thursday, to pay Maudie a pre-Christmas visit. Please will you and Roland come for supper on Wednesday?'

Belinda was in the stables helping Victoria to prepare the loose boxes when Jack called her to come back to the house. Lettice wanted an urgent word with her on the telephone.

'I can't understand. A note has come from Victoria saying that Archie and Harold are going to stay in your stables. What they must think I daren't imagine. It beggars description. The presumption of inviting them when she hardly knows them, and to such discomfort, exceeds all limits. Poor dears are obviously anxious that it would hurt my feelings were they to refuse. It has put everyone in a terrible position.'

'I don't think it was meant to be presumptuous. They want to see Maudie – being godfathers.'

'They can do that perfectly well from here. I'm inclined to ring Archie – I know him so well – and suggest that they stay with us in comfort and visit Maudie during the day. Not that he likes babies.'

'You must do what you think best. Perhaps I gave Victoria too much encouragement – at least as far as accommodation in the stables. I remembered you once saying that, being cerebral, Archie Thorne was adaptable to surroundings. I repeated it to her to boost her courage.'

'It doesn't sound to me as if it needs much boosting. It's plain cheek on her part and I have every right to be angry.'

Archie answered the telephone. There was another man in the room; a colleague who had come by appointment to ask for suggestions. He wanted to extricate himself from a boring marriage and Archie was saying, 'But first you have to tell me a great deal more,' when it rang. He made an impatient gesture to show his guest that no incoming call was to distract him from the boringness of his marriage.

'Archie. I hail and greet thee.' Lettice's voice.

'I'm awfully sorry. I can't make out what you're saying or, indeed, who you can be. Would you terribly mind ringing me some other time?'

He put the receiver down and said, 'Of course you are in a very difficult position. She seems to have been a most considerate wife.'

Lettice, dashed by Archie's abruptness, wondered if Harold had ever used a telephone. He might shed some light. She asked the college to connect her with his room. He heard the bell ring but did not cross the room to answer it.

An hour and a half later Archie, after detailed questioning, wound up the interview.

'How easy it is to give advice,' he said. 'You are going to think me very harsh. It seems to me that your wife has done nothing more terrible than habitually to spread a length of pink satin, which she refers to as a *cache linge* over the chair in your bedroom on which she places her underwear at night. Of course my advice must, naturally, be disregarded but have you ever thought of providing her with a dressing room?'

Again the telephone rang.

The *cache-linge* victim made his getaway as Archie hurried to answer Lettice's second attempt.

'Archie. It's an age since we spoke. Great news that we shall see the New Year in together once again.'

'I'm much looking forward to it. So is Harold.'

'Friendship is so important. Funny – how it matters.'

'Indeed. Quite right.'

'One other thing. I hear from Victoria that you are going to stay in the stables. Can it be true?'

'Indeed. Can I count on seeing you there?'

'Archie. Don't go. I know you do it to please me and I am deeply touched.'

'Of course. I would always want to please you but why shouldn't we go?'

'It will be hideously uncomfortable. I don't know how she has the nerve to suggest it. Grief can do odd things to people. God knows – we have suffered ourselves.'

'I'm terribly sorry. You have been wonderful. Don't add to your worries by thinking of my comfort. We will simply arm ourselves with extra clothing.'

'It's not only the cold. I think it's unsuitable.'

'Ah. Now I see. Let me put your mind at rest. Harold is included in the invitation so there is no question of impropriety.'

Chapter 7

The journey had seemed long to both of them. Archie drove his Daimler up the rutted drive and stopped outside the stable block that ran across one side of a courtyard facing Jack and Belinda's farmhouse. He put down two identical suitcases beside a new doormat and rang the bell. Harold followed carrying a small book.

Victoria opened the door.

'I'm glad you've arrived, both of you. Lettice and Roland are coming this evening. Jack has given me some wine.'

'Good. But this is very nice. Harold has never slept in a stable before and is terribly excited. Harold, tell Victoria what you said on the way here.'

'No. No. Not now. Some other time.'

Victoria led them further in.

'Are we going to sleep in mangers?' Archie asked.

At suppertime Lettice's head, encased in a tricorn hat, peered around the door. Roland followed, smiling.

Victoria opened the door to her parents-in-law and followed them into the room where the reunion took place.

Lettice removed a blue veil and greeted Victoria's guests. 'What fun this is. Victoria is brave to start entertaining so soon. It is still all we can do to drag ourselves out. Young people are so resilient compared to our sensitive generation.'

Lettice, a trifle breathless, extended stiff arms towards Victoria. 'You darling. I so nearly bought you the most exquisite remnant of Victorian beadwork in the marketplace today. I was drooling in front of that lovely shop "All Our Yesterdays" and a beam of colour caught my eye. An enchanting scrap. Perfect example of the patience we women have, sadly, allowed to slip away in these frenzied, servant-less days.' By the time she stopped, Lettice was more than a trifle breathless and Victoria hesitated before answering. Was she supposed to thank Lettice for this piece of near-generosity? Was it, in fact, the thought that counted?

'Oh,' she answered, cautiously confused. 'You shouldn't have.'

'I didn't. I mean, I did want to but the expense was too beastly. It was heaven. A million beads and stitches. It would have been perfect on that damp bit of wall by the chimney-piece.'

Archie said, 'I think you are all perfectly wonderful. I shall take it upon myself to pour out drinks. Lettice, I know you don't.'

He handed a weak drink to Roland and a strong one to Harold as Lettice's eyes danced around the room. Annoyance rose to fury as she took stock of comforts provided by Belinda.

The men drank whisky as Victoria sat down beside Lettice and apologised in advance for the dinner.

'Dearest. You should have asked me to help. As you know I am a natural cook. I maintain that cooking is a creative art – closely related to sculpture – and must never be allowed to become a chore. Ask Archie. Food is constantly referred to in literature.'

They ate in the kitchen. Lettice writhed. 'This has been a year of great sadness. How happy Edgar would be if he knew, and I say this in particular to Archie and Harold, how my friends have rallied around Victoria.'

Archie told them both the story of his colleague and the *cache linge*. Victoria said, 'What about a dressing room?'

'Characteristically,' he said. 'Characteristically you have put your finger on it. Lettice. Roland. Your daughter-in-law is remarkably sharp.'

Lettice, out of control, shrieked, 'So sharp she'll cut herself.'

Soon after dinner she and Roland took their leave. 'You must all come to us tomorrow. If you are weary, Victoria darling, send the men over. They ought to know the way.'

Archie said that he would ring Lettice in the morning.

'So. It's hail and farewell,' she answered with wistful hardness.

Harold went straight to his stall and fell onto the bed where he slept without removing his clothes.

Archie and Victoria talked into the night. They drank wine as he complained of feeling old and raged against the abolition of capital punishment.

When, the next day, the two men called at The Old Keep,

they found Lettice alone in the garden room, hair wrapped in a gingham scarf and clothes protected by a painter's smock as she squirted silver paint over a branch of holly.

'You've caught me at what I call my dreadful decorations.' She put down her spray gun.

'Don't let us disturb you. Harold, isn't she marvellous? Is all this connected with Christmas celebrations?'

'Isn't it shaming? I don't think I'll ever grow out of my child-like excitement at Christmas time.'

'You mustn't. Don't attempt to.'

Harold pressed a finger onto the wet leaves. He wiped the paint off with a red and white spotted handkerchief thrust at him by Archie.

Lettice looked into his face. 'I can see that Harold is every bit as bad as me. There's nothing as tantalising as wet paint, but *quel cafard* if we had to be adult all the time.'

A narrow passage, paved in flagstones, connected the flower room with a forsaken day nursery. Lettice was engaged in turning it into a scribbling and daubing den for herself.

'Then the beastes goe into their dennes and remain in their places.' She explained how it was spelled as they looked about. 'Book of Job.'

Archie and Harold sat on a bench, one extracted by Lettice from an abandoned church, and debated on the desirability of dennes.

Archie introduced the sore subject. 'We are much enjoying our stay at the stables. I hope it isn't too tiring for Victoria.'

'Quite honestly it would serve her right if she dropped.'

Lettice let a cascade of abuse flood over her hearers. They cajoled and reprehended her in turn. Harold shrank in pain as he noticed shadows of anility cross Lettice's face.

Archie, appointing himself professor, transformed the scene into a seminar. 'Perhaps we should go back and examine the situation from the beginning.'

Harold checked him. 'No, Archie, not now. No. No. Some other time.'

They left The Old Keep, conversation unsuccessfully concluded, without remembering to greet Roland.

'Should we explore the representation of each?'

'No. No. I think it would be unwise to give encouragement.'

'Are you, with your extraordinary insight, trying to point out that they, neither of them, have anything of interest to say?'

'Not precisely. No. I wouldn't say that.'

'Perhaps you are hinting at something of the sort. We have noticed that Lettice and Victoria are both women.'

'My thoughts were connected with that knowledge.'

'If we were wise we would go straight back to Cambridge and not communicate again with either of them.'

'I don't think that would show wisdom.'

Harold was thinking, in part, of the few possessions he had left in Victoria's care. He did not want to lose the small book.

'Of course. You are right. Nonetheless, it is a frightful nuisance – the whole thing.'

'That didn't occur to you until you went too far and upset Lettice.'

Chapter 8

Victoria had been in a state of undefined bliss. Apart from Lettice's lapse during dinner, Archie and Harold's visit was perfect. Beyond all hope.

After Roland and Lettice left the evening before and Harold had crept off to bed, Victoria and Archie stayed up talking until Maudie cried soon after five o'clock. Never before had a human creature been capable of removing the burdens of daily existence from her mind.

So, when the two men returned from the outing from which she had extricated herself, she was slow to notice any change in Archie.

It wasn't possible that her wise, distracting friend of the night before could alter without warning.

When Archie's peevishness became apparent her suspicion fell on Harold's scarcely hidden jealousy. Lettice, she was certain, held no power.

'I hope you haven't arranged anything for this afternoon,'

Archie spat. 'I, for one, intend to sleep. You kept me up far too late.'

His expression was mean and old-maidish; appearance distorted. The battle between the women was more than he could cope with.

Victoria took refuge in the kitchen. She stood back, hands against the distempered wall, spreading and flattening them, palms downwards, onto the paint behind her. She hoped that rising damp might cool the heat of her body. Then she turned from left to right placing first one hot cheek and then the other against the powdery wall.

Harold ate fast and wandered off before lunch was finished. Archie made no effort to be polite until he saw tears forming in Victoria's eyes. As they ran over her cheekbones, he handed her his red spotted handkerchief – clean but for a silver fingerprint.

'Does it enrage you to see a woman cry?'

'Not in all cases. I would be sympathetic to the sight of a mother, say, crying over the death of her child.'

'What about a father?'

He decided to charm her before resting. It would not take long. He went to her side. She hadn't noticed Harold's silver fingerprint on Archie's handkerchief and tucked it away for future tears.

After her guests left Victoria waited for Lettice to ring.

'Darling. Have they gone? A relief for one and all, I should imagine. I thought Archie was very difficult. Not at all his old self.'

'It's hard for me to say.'

'Of course. Impossible. To us, knowing him as we do, the change was very noticeable. All that flattery is quite new.'

'I think he was unwell.'

'I can't say that I suspected any such thing. Did he mention it?'

'No. Not at all.'

'There you are. He would have been sure to tell me if anything had been the matter.'

Back in Cambridge, Archie rang Victoria.

'Just to let you know that we arrived safely. It was wonderful being with you. Harold is almost embarrassing in his praise of you. Quite rightly. You must visit us here after the New Year which, as you know, we are to spend at The Old Keep. We will certainly meet then. I will ring you again in a day or two.'

His voice was tired and the pitch high. She asked him if he was unwell.

'You are very perceptive. I am not well. I sleep badly at night and can't concentrate fully during the day. I realise that I'm getting old. My body feels old and the mechanical parts of my brain. I do forget everything. However, I won't forget you or Maudie.'

Four days later, a letter arrived for Victoria from Harold. After thanking her for the nights he had spent at the stables, he went on to say, 'Archie is rather unwell. I doubt if there is any cause for anxiety. He spent the day in bed yesterday but refused to send for the doctor or to take his temperature. I will let you know of any developments – good or bad.'

Harold was assiduous in providing Victoria with bulletins and rang her the day after his letter had arrived.

'I regret having given you any cause for alarm about Archie. He is not really ill but very tired. There seem to be a large number of administrative jobs to do with the running of the college which are proving complicated and unpleasant.'

'I'd love to see him. Would you let me know if he would like a visit?'

'Yes. Of course. Most certainly. I will ring you again, if I may.'

'Thank you. You are kind.'

'No. No. Not at all. Not in the least.'

── Chapter 9 ──

Victoria took Maudie to lunch at The Old Keep on Christmas Day. She would have liked to stay at home but Belinda advised her to go 'particularly this year'.

Maudie was wrapped in a thick red shawl ready for the expedition when Harold rang. Planting her on the floor, Victoria answered the telephone.

'I want to tell you that Archie is now rather ill. The doctor, being cautious, has sent him to hospital. He says that it may be pneumonia. I don't think there is any reason to worry and he is in extremely good hands.'

Harold gave her the name and address of the hospital that lay outside the city and where Archie had been sent the evening before.

'I think a letter would be welcome. He is very depressed.'

Victoria wrote, quickly, before setting off.

'Dearest Archie. I can't bear you being ill. Please get better soon and remember how much we love you. What a horrible

Christmas. I hope you don't get bothered by balloons and communion wine. I wish I could see you. I'm knitting you a scarf.'

Pulling a tartan cape trimmed with velvet ribbons over her shoulder, Lettice descended the tower steps. Forcing her arms through each gap, she stretched them towards the baby. 'Let me take the precious bundle.'

They stood for a moment in the hall under a bunch of silver holly – removing coats and shawls. Lettice wore a shimmering Christmas frock. It came down from its hanger once a year and was worn throughout the special day. Roland looked at his life partner and thought she had bags of spirit. No one can deny that.

Lettice gave Victoria a lute in trust for Maudie. 'It was my lute. Especially designed for me by a famous lute-maker. I used to play and sing to it.'

Alice picked the baby up and searched for signs of emotional disturbance.

Shortly before lunch, Lettice warned, 'I'm going to ring Archie. We always talk on Christmas Day.'

Victoria, unable to bring herself to admit that she knew he was in hospital, asked, 'Where?'

'He's sure to be at his lodgings. He always lunches *en famille* at Christmas. Probably some of his cousins and Harold. The usual, you know.'

She was gone, down the passage to the telephone and dialling furiously.

Back and mystified she said, 'Very bizarre. No reply,' glancing at Victoria who had got out her knitting and was making a scarf for Archie. 'Did he say anything – *en passant* I mean, when he stayed with you?'

'No. He didn't mention his Christmas plans then.'

'Since? Has he mentioned them since?'

Joanna bounced in, 'You're not still talking about that prickly old Thorne, are you? He's biting into your flesh.' Pleased with her joke she turned to Victoria.

'The baby's spiffing but don't you find her an awful bind?'

Signalling in lively fashion, Lettice led the party along a festooned hall.

'Victoria. You must sit by me, then Maudie will be near the fire.'

'I'll feed Maudie. It won't kill me for once.' Joanna, with wisdom unexpected in one so young and brash, saw danger in seating her mother next to Victoria who quickly exchanged seats. Victoria longed to get on with the complicated pattern she knitted into Archie's scarf and which was bundled into her bag.

The meal over, a restless and fidgety Lettice said, 'I'll try Archie again. It was silly of me not to remember. Often they go out for a drink before luncheon on Christmas Day. And, Roland, don't forget to give Orpheus some special delicacies on this of all days.'

Chapter 10

Harold, having eaten alone in an expensive hotel, went to Archie's study at the lodgings.

He turned on a bar of the electric fire. There were things that Archie might like to have with him in hospital. He sat down on an armchair, still wearing a black overcoat, while his mind went round and round. He was organising an operation.

When the telephone rang he shuddered from shock.

It could only be Archie or, more alarming, news from the hospital. He took the receiver and held it with a damp hand as a voice said, 'All form of Christmas nonsense from The Old Keep. Don't say you have overindulged and rendered yourself silent. What pagan feasts you do go in for.'

'No. It's Harold. I'm sorry. Archie can't, I'm afraid. Not now. Oh dear. I'm sorry.'

'What did I say? I'm always telling him that he's just a motherless boy at heart. I'll have a word with him, sober or otherwise.'

'No. He can't. He really can't. He's rather bad. Ill, I mean. Rather ill. I was fetching some things.'

Lettice capped the mouthpiece and cried, loud and clear down the passage, 'Archie's ill.' Uncupping, she wailed, 'I'm sorry. I wish I'd known. Does anyone know – besides yourself, I mean?'

She squinted as she thought with sour suspicion of Victoria.

'There hasn't been much time. It was only yesterday. He went to hospital yesterday. I was going to let you know.'

'I won't be cross but, another time, you must do so at once. That's what friends are for and, as I said to Archie the other day, friendship is so important. One needs to remember this more and more with the sad changes that go on around us.'

'Oh dear. Of course. I know. I'm sorry. Oh dear.'

'Don't be hard on yourself. You shall come for the New Year whatever happens. Even if poor Archie can't make it. I'll have to say that you rang me instead of the other way round or it would look bad.'

Near to fainting, Harold sat down and wound a greasy curl around his thumb. How kind of Lettice to accept him, alone if necessary, for the New Year.

Lettice, tense with humiliation, returned to the sitting room and broke the news of Archie's illness.

Joanna started to sing.

Poor old Archie Thorne
Soon we'll have to mourn
Hope he doesn't yawn
When the thread is shorn

Unabashed by her stupefied audience, she continued.

Poor old Archie Thorne
Soon be dead and gorne.

'Joanna. Go to your room. Stay there. Stay there for the rest of the day. Roland. Send her away.'

Victoria gathered up Maudie and said that she had to return the car to Belinda. She was desperate to finish the scarf.

In the evening, Joanna's father insisted she should be released from her room.

'Christmas comes but once a year,' he reminded them.

'After the way she behaved. On this day of all days. I know that youth will have its way – but disrespect is something else. This once I will give in and we'll all try to remember somebody else who knew how to forgive.'

When allowed down, Joanna said, 'I'm terribly sorry. It's just that I've got a bit sick of hearing about him. I mean – it's been going on all my life and now Victoria has caught the bug. But it's awful that he's ill.'

Lettice, well rehearsed, admonished, 'I want you to learn, mark and inwardly digest this, Joanna. I am not the only one to notice – they said the same in your school report – that sometimes you forget that there are such people as your elders and betters. Archie definitely comes into this category and so, I hope, do I. Not that I recognise the generation gap.'

Wearied by her speech she sank back into the faded pattern of her chair cover.

Alice dwelled, 'It's odd how people with exactly the same background can turn out so very different.'

Roland patted her head and said, 'Clever girl.'

No news of Archie came either to The Old Keep or to the stables until the following day.

Harold rang Lettice. 'There has been a marked improvement but he is very weak. Very weak indeed.'

'Any hope for the New Year?'

'I don't know. I don't know.'

'Keep me *au fait* and don't forget that you are welcome, even on your own.'

'I'm sure Archie would like a letter.' He gave her the hospital address.

Lettice wrote, 'We are all distracted. Fond messages from Alice and Joanna – as from Roland and myself – that goes without saying. What can one say? Don't allow yourself to worry about the New Year. I have promised Harold he shall come *n'importe quoi* and I am going to be very firm about your recuperation. You are to come here as soon as you are let out.'

Harold rang Victoria. 'There has been a marked improvement but he is very weak. Very weak indeed.'

Before getting better Archie got worse and Harold continued to inform both Lettice and Victoria. He rang them each day and provided them with the same information and Victoria, fearing outbursts, allowed Lettice to believe she broke the news.

'Too sweet. Dear Harold rings every evening. He knows how important we are to Archie and I've promised to hand all information on to you.'

──Chapter 11──

Archie, from his bed, was gentle. Victoria, exhausted after a long drive, sat beside him as he promised to talk to Lettice on the telephone. 'Far better that I should tell her myself that you have visited me – or have I spoken to her already? We won't think about it again. Poor Lettice. Beneath it all she has a kind heart though not, I think, a very warm one.'

'You forget things on purpose.'

'But of course.'

'Could you explain her for me again? Like you did after Roland's exhibition. As far as I'm concerned she's foul.'

'Shall I try? I did warn you not to expect me at my best either physically or intellectually.'

'I'm selfish. Let's leave it until you're better.'

'As you say. Try to remember one thing though. You have had a terrible time and you expect others to have courage equal to your own. You make no allowance for an important and una-voidable fact. That of age. There are differences between the problems of the young and the problems of the not so young. Now. Tell me about Christmas. Was it perfectly frightful?'

'Fairly bad.'

'Did you admire the Christmas dress?'

They laughed until Archie coughed.

Harold appeared at the foot of the bed and told them that it was late.

Tears splashed as she drove home. It took her six hours.

She went to the farmhouse in the morning to thank Belinda for her help and to reclaim Maudie. Belinda told her of their disagreeable evening at The Old Keep and advised, 'Jack says you must ignore her. Her jealous outbreaks are too pathetic to be taken seriously. Terror of being left out consumes her. I know how it can feel but I react differently. At first I get cross, but then I sort of fizzle out.'

'I'll try,' Victoria said, 'but it's going to be uphill work.'

The day before, Lettice had told Victoria that there was not a hope for the New Year. 'He's not even well enough for visitors. Apart from Harold.'

Jack and Belinda had been expected to dine with Lettice and Roland on New Year's Eve – an unusual concession when outside visitors were staying in the house. Lettice rang Belinda.

'I've completely lost heart about the New Year. It seems cruel to celebrate without Archie. Come and have a cosy evening here – just ourselves – before then.

They went and Lettice made several points.

'We've never thanked you both properly for all you have done for Victoria and the babe. I've been almost guilty of burying the subject for fear that it might be proving too much for you both. She's such a strange girl.'

'We love having her and to feel that the stables are being used.'

'Do you find her – what shall I say – a little unfathomable?'

'No. Not at all. She's wonderful.'

'It's known to be a difficult relationship – mother and daughter-in-law. You wait till your Arthur gets married! Of course it's twice as difficult for me without the irreplaceable link.'

Thinking of his dead son and of the two Bobbies, Roland spoke, 'It's not as though she'd taken our granddaughter away.'

Decorations were left over from Christmas.

Lettice, peeping through a table arrangement of crisp dried flowers, asked, 'Where has she gone? I tried to ring her several times today and drew a complete blank. Do you know, either of you, where she might be?'

Arthur's old nurse was staying at Jack and Belinda's farmhouse and had, once again, taken charge of Maudie for the day while Victoria drove to the sick bed.

The daffodil trilled. 'That will be Harold. He always rings at this time with news of Archie.'

It was Archie himself.

'At last,' he said. 'At last, like Edward the Eighth, I can say a few words for myself. But only just.' He broke off and coughed. 'I'm sorry. What a perfectly frightful noise. I simply can't help it.'

'Don't try to stop. Cough it up. I mean to say – have your cough. I'll wait as long as you like.'

'That's better. And I'm better. At least I think I am. I was cheered by my visitor today. What a wonderful girl Victoria is!'

Lettice, near prostration, moaned, 'How good of you. You shouldn't have let her in. Somebody should protect you.'

'Protect me from enjoying myself?'

'From visitors.'

'Oh surely not. She's the first I've had apart from Harold. I needed distraction and simply suggested she should come.'

Lettice struggled along and repeatedly reminded him of her invitation for his recuperation.

'It is very kind,' he answered. 'I shall have to see. Can I let you know? I will tell you as soon as I possibly can.'

Seated, Lettice peered at Belinda through the flower arrangement. 'Did you know where she had gone? Who's looking after Maudie? Why didn't you say?'

'I was going to when the telephone went.'

Two days later a letter came for Victoria from Archie.

'I cannot tell you how much good you did me. Aren't you wonderful! I had almost forgotten how wonderful you were! Almost but not quite. The evening of the day that you came I was told that I could go back to the lodgings where I now am. I love the scarf and am immensely touched that you should have made it for me. I admire your skill. I get up early before breakfast and put it on with my dressing gown and walk about my bedroom and sitting room wearing it, as I am doing now – apart from walking. Your constant sympathy is keeping me alive – but only just. I have been given some pills to send me to sleep – not permanently of course. Against all principles I have decided to take them. The nights have been perfectly horrid. Lettice is being relentless about my convalescence; reminding me constantly of the value of friendship. It looks as if I am to be transported to The Old Keep, willynilly, in a week or so. Can I rely on seeing you there daily?'

A week later, they were transported, willy-nilly, in a hired car to The Old Keep.

Archie was sent, immediately, to his room and, as he looked about, wondered if he was in his right mind. He called for Harold – wanting a second opinion. A fire glowed in a small hearth. That was not all. By his bed, on a Regency whatnot, he thought he saw a bottle of whisky, a reel of white cotton – needle piercing it at right angles – a torch, matches, biscuits and other objects that his mind could not absorb.

Harold smiled. 'Isn't Lettice wonderful. Musical sheets have even been set out at the pianola.'

Lettice approached. 'Can I come in – just to see if needs are answered.' There was an electric kettle under her arm.

'Needs I never knew of. Aren't you marvellous.'

'I suddenly thought of a kettle.'

'I could have muddled through without one. What does Harold say?'

'Surely yes. Surely you could. You always do.'

'Aren't bachelors bliss! Everybody needs an electric kettle. What if you want to refill your hotty in the middle of the night?'

'My what?'

'Hotty. Hot-water bottle. We always call them hotties. A family expression.'

'Very well. I shall accept your offer and refill my hotty.'

At Belinda's stables Victoria blinked and swallowed as she pictured Archie so near – settling in.

Rushing it, Lettice had said, 'Not a mouse shall cross the threshold until I give the all-clear.'

Harold retired early in the evening and Archie drank three quarters of the contents of the whisky bottle – helping down a sleeping pill.

The next day, Lettice told Harold that the country air was already doing Archie good. 'Midday and he's still asleep.'

At lunchtime he emerged and said he was feeling the benefit.

'The fare is going to be simple. Vital after illness. No concessions to gracious living.'

'Is your daughter-in-law going to visit us?'

Squint-eyed, Lettice replied, 'No exceptions for a day or two.' Cautious when Archie didn't reply she, with every nerve aflame, said, 'But why not ring her up?'

'Later on. Is this boiled fish?'

'As the doctor himself would have ordered.'

That night Archie found that the bottle, one third full of whisky, had been replaced by a full one. Drinking more than he had done the night before, his pill slipped down easily.

A day or two went by. Harold walked in the woods and Archie barely surfaced.

With Archie close by but kept at bay, Victoria, gripped with misery, took her tears to Belinda. Dabbing at them with the red spotted rag, she asked what to do.

'Nothing, of course.' Victoria smiled. Belinda said, 'You may think me very harsh but there is nothing you can do.'

'Can't I send a note?'

'He'll know why you don't – if you don't.'

'He'd ignore that.'

'Not entirely. Only to avoid trouble. Certainly to the extent of not contacting you while he's staying with Lettice.'

Then, taking pity, Belinda said, 'But I'll ring her. Just to enquire. I'll leave you out of it.'

Victoria was furiously angry. Archie should have warned or protected her. Perhaps she had been unimaginative but he had given encouragement and had never advised her to exercise restraint.

Before dialling, Belinda warned, 'Don't hope for much.'

Lettice, racing to answer, told Archie, 'I wish I'd had it disconnected while you were here.'

'Not on my account, I hope. However, since you didn't, I won't fuss.'

Lettice lost his words as she answered Belinda's call. 'How kind. I meant to ring you but all my energies have been taken up with nursing.' Then, silencing Archie, 'Virtue is getting her reward. Roses are beginning to blossom on his cheeks again.'

It was true that Archie's colour was unnaturally high. He felt extremely ill and planned to discuss the matter with Harold at the earliest opportunity.

In the fully furnished bedroom, he sat down near the window and convulsed into coughing.

'It's no good. A doctor must be called.' White with worry, Harold went to Lettice. 'Is there a doctor? A good one? Archie is unwell.'

'Why didn't he say?'

'He did. A minute ago. Can you call one, please?'

A feeble jangle came from the cowbell in Archie's room. Harold mounted the stairs, taking them in threes. During the seconds that had passed since clasping the bell, Archie had fallen asleep. The pianola vibrated in rhythm with his snores.

Harold sat beside him until a car drew up.

The doctor, unfamiliar with his patient, insisted that Archie be returned to hospital. 'It could be pleurisy,' he said. 'Also, this is a little awkward. Does he drink to excess?'

Harold hustled him out. Rain had been pouring down since daybreak and the roads were wet.

Archie, horizontal, and Harold, upright, spent what seemed like hours in the ambulance.

Victoria, in the wet, pushed Maudie's pram along the farm track towards a wider road. She jumped at the noise of a hooter. Lettice's car advanced. Stopping, she wound the window down and popped a plumed head through the gap.

'I was en route for the stables. Pining for a chat.'

Victoria had to walk back with Maudie. It would only take ten minutes. They would meet up at the stables.

'What a fiasco,' Lettice wailed when they were reunited. 'Archie has been borne away in an ambulance.'

As had often happened to Lettice's victims, Victoria found, quite suddenly, that she had lost the will to struggle.

'The doctor rang me after they'd left and suggested that Archie was drunk. I have trained Lily to see that there's always a whisky bottle by the spare-room bed but only today did I discover that she had been replacing Archie's each morning.' Lettice began to sob and, as she sobbed, she threw herself about on the sofa.

Victoria, dry-eyed, handed her Archie's filthy handkerchief saying, quietly, 'You can keep it. Keep it as long as you like.'

Part Four

Chapter 1

It was a few weeks later and Archie, apart from the ill effects of sporadic drinking bouts, was in excellent health.

'Harold. Isn't it time we asked Victoria here once again?'

'If you say so.'

'You were very full of her praises.'

'Indeed.'

'Do you have to be so heavy?'

'No. No. By all means. Let her come.'

'Lettice has subsided and I'd enjoy it.'

Archie wrote. 'A lot of fluid has passed through my lungs since we spoke. I am now rather well and wish to entertain you here. So does Harold.'

Victoria had been feeling low and accepted at once. A packet had come for her accompanied by a note from Mungo. 'One thinks one mentioned that one wanted you to have a little keepsake. Something that belonged to Laurence. One has pondered a lot on the question and has stumbled on something appropriate. This watercolour that you so skilfully created. One admits that it is a wrench for one to part with it but feel that it should, by right, be yours. One's sorry that one had to remove the frame. Perhaps one day, if you are ever in these parts, you might like to collect it.'

What had happened to Laurence's stepdaughter, the Comtessa Primrose? Had she been cut out of his will?

Archie and Harold prepared for Victoria's visit. 'Harold. What are we to do about this?' He slid a summons from a renowned and neighbouring hostess, Perdita Chanter, over the table. 'In view of the situation we should either propose taking Victoria with us or we should decline to go. Which do you advise?'

'That depends.'

'What on?'

'On you. On how you behave.'

Archie chuckled, 'We shall take her.'

Leaving Maudie with Arthur's old nurse, Victoria travelled on a series of trains to Cambridge.

Archie wrote to Perdita Chanter. 'You have heard me speak of Victoria Holliday. The widow of Roland and Lettice Holliday's son, Edgar. She will be spending the weekend here and I write to ask if we can bring her with us to your luncheon party.'

On opening the letter, Perdita Chanter pressed a button on one of three telephones and dialled the number of the painter, Robert Stratton.

'Tell me everything you know about Victoria Holliday.'

'She used to live with Laurence. Laurence Bland in Italy. I met her there once or twice. Very talented painter, I thought.'

'Go on.'

'I was disappointed when she married that dreary Edgar.'

'She's Archie's new friend. He's bringing her here and I want some background. For heaven's sake, go on.'

'Well. She used to be frightfully pretty. Buxom. On the plump side.'

'Not huge bosoms?'

'They were a fair size.'

'That's terribly funny. Archie's always hated bosoms. He's got a thing about them.'

Robert had to hurry.

Later, in Victoria's presence, Archie demanded of Harold, 'I wonder what Victoria will make of Perdita.'

'I don't know. I couldn't say.'

'Women. She doesn't like women.' He was talking of Perdita.

'How foul,' Victoria pouted and cracked her knuckles as Archie winced.

'I would be surprised if this time she doesn't make an exception.'

Victoria was nervous in the front of the Daimler. Archie never made use of the driving mirror and her fears increased as the hostess, on their arrival, stared at the front of her jacket before saying a word.

The room was full of people; mostly men. Perdita wore her hair in a bun; out of joint with the rest of her elegant appearance. A skilled social technician, she whirled Victoria towards the runt of the group; a mossy youth sent by a firm of London auctioneers to put a price on Perdita's possessions. Smoking,

Perdita drawled to Archie, 'I hope the merry widow can hold her own.'

Victoria could barely hold her glass.

She was placed between the assessor and a prosperous young man; the very one that Lettice had provided for Alice after Roland's exhibition. The assessor told her how stimulating it was to work amongst beautiful things.

'One or two mouth-watering possessions here.' He lowered his voice.

Perdita, celebrated for having reintroduced general conversation after the war, craned across her neighbour and addressed Victoria as though to disembowel her.

'Archie tells me that Henry, next to you, knows your parents-in-law somehow or other.'

Victoria turned to him and introduced the topic.

'Not really,' he said, 'but your mother-in-law does keep ringing me up and asking me to things. I was invited to a dinner she gave not long ago at the Ritz after some exhibition. She's relentless. I hope that I don't sound rude.'

Archie, on Perdita's left and fairly far from Victoria, said, 'Aren't you wonderful. You've started her off.'

'Now we shall have to see if she knows when to stop. I hope to God she doesn't bang on about those ghastly Hollidays throughout lunch.'

Archie arranged an expression of timidity as he heaped a white and curly pinnacle onto his plate. Perdita said, 'Ordered for the occasion. It's called Widow's Peak.'

'Is that supposed to be a joke?'

Perdita said that it was time for general conversation.

'Now. I know we're all wondering which coward wrote that ambiguous review about Roy's book in the *TLS*.'

On the way back to Cambridge Archie said, 'Poor Perdita. She's a bit of a goose but a very human one, if such a thing is possible.'

To Victoria, 'Harold thinks I should marry her.'

'Why?'

'He likes her. She's always been very good about including him in her invitations although he never utters and contributes nothing.'

Harold had been mistaken. Archie was capable, after all, of saying things bad enough to make Victoria hate him. She, concerned for Harold's feelings, turned and put her hand over the back of her seat, letting it rest by the knob of the pull-out picnic table behind her. Harold took it in his and they travelled on in silence and in some danger.

Harold went to his room.

Dining with Victoria, Archie questioned, 'Did I notice a birdlike hand claw yours when we were in the car?'

'You were certainly in a position to notice what was going on behind you.'

'Are you criticising my driving?'

'No. Just remarking.'

'Very well. You haven't answered my question.'

'Then. Yes.'

'But this is wonderful. It's so frightfully good for him. I don't see him holding Lettice's hand – or Perdita's.'

'Perhaps you wouldn't talk as you did in front of them. Poor Harold. You made him sound delinquent – saying it was good of Perdita to include him.'

'Are you upbraiding me?'

'Mildly.'

Later on he said, 'I think I despise you.'

Wistful for the spotted handkerchief and wishing she hadn't given it to Lettice, Victoria asked, 'What for? How dare you? What for?'

'For taking it all to heart.'

Only half in jest, she shouted, 'Humbug. Twisted, flint-hearted hypocrite. Tormented misogynist. Pedant, quack and sham.' She was a bit drunk.

'I would go and fetch you a drink but I don't want to miss anything that you might say in my absence.'

They were interrupted by a shrill ring from the telephone.

'Perdita here. I was fascinated to meet the Holliday widow. I can see the whole thing.'

'What thing are you referring to?'

'Your thing about her. She's frightfully attractive and what a frontispiece! Now. Seriously. I want you to help raise money for me to save the nation. There's a strong note of feminine hysteria in our funds office and I've given your name as somebody who'll help.'

'I'm terribly busy at the moment. I'll ring you back.'

Perdita lay down and called out, 'Do fetch me a toddy, Nanny. God I wish people would stop changing horses mid-stream.'

Harold crept into Archie's bed that night and told him that

he was in love with Victoria but intended to allow his feelings to remain unexpressed, if possible, for ever.

Archie, applauding each decision, for he regarded both as such, said, 'This is all perfectly wonderful.'

He had noticed that Perdita was a little captivated by Victoria and probably planned to take her up.

Chapter 2

Before going to sleep, Harold, stronger than Archie now, leant across the narrow bed and hit the other on the eye.

The next day, a large area of Archie's face showed bruising. In parts the skin had broken. He made weak attempts at concealment, applying a number of small sticky plasters. At breakfast a horrified Victoria ordered him to sit. She peeled off the plasters as Archie shrank.

'Of course this is very good of you,' he said, voice high-pitched.

With incredible pliancy she ran to a chemist shop where she bought a tube of cosmetic cream.

When the treatment was finished he looked passable, albeit mottled, and Victoria returned to the stables.

Perdita called, unexpectedly, on Archie that afternoon. She needed his advice and a signature. He signed with a flourish as she saw his face and sniffed.

Later she rang the college bursar with whom she had always

managed to stay on close terms. 'It must be more passionate than we guessed. The widow has given him a black eye, and that's not all. He's allowed her to camouflage the wounds with reeking face cream. We must investigate.'

Robert Stratton, the socially ubiquitous painter, rang Victoria.

'It's far too long since we met and I've been hearing the terrible tale of Archie Thorne's black eye.'

'Heavens! Poor Archie.'

'I'm glad it was that way round. You might have been killed if he'd given you one.'

'Given me what?'

'A black eye. You must be stronger than you look.'

'What can you be saying?'

'Everybody knows. The town crier has informed the cabinet.'

Victoria suggested that they meet. 'I promise not to cause you any bodily harm.'

Archie rang Victoria. 'This is simply to say how much I appreciated your invaluable assistance. The damage went undetected, thanks to your skills.'

'Not entirely, I hear. In parliament today I was held responsible for abrasions.'

'Once again, I hope you don't expect me to understand one word of what you say.'

Robert Stratton planned to give a party. Perdita rang him. 'I hope to God the widow won't be there.'

'Why?'

'I can't stand fisticuffs.'

'Has anyone asked you to?'

'Not yet but I can always smell an imbroglio.'

She rang Archie and put the same point. He answered, 'Victoria is certain to be there. Indeed, both Harold and I hope to see her.'

'We'd better get Robert to put "knuckle-dusters" on the card.'

'You know the invitations have already been dispatched.'

'It's terribly tiresome not knowing anything about her background. I can usually tell unless people are arty or foreign. I believe her mother was Norwegian or some such nationality.'

'Will you be going yourself in view of all this nonsense?'

'Willy-nilly,' Perdita stopped to smoke and to cough.

Robert, on hearing further whispers of unrest, called the party off.

After pressing a button, Perdita dialled. 'Long to know why you've funked it. Is it something to do with the widow? Has she hidden her mite under a bushel or something? Perhaps it would be better if she did.'

Robert, strict, told her, 'As you know, I'm very fond of Victoria but I'm also very bored of hearing about her. Sorry about the party. I've been called away. Say what you like.'

'How about Tit Widow?'

Nobody wanted to join in. That was the greatest hurdle to be climbed.

Left to herself she had one more try and wrote:

There once was a widow who knew
How to hand out a black eye or two.
As well as her thrust, she'd a pendulous bust…

'Oh hell. I seem to have lost my touch. Perhaps I'd better give up smoking.'

She dropped her pen, drained of poison, and walked about a bit.

Her old nurse said, 'Think of your first wedding and how the whole village was given a half-holiday.'

Chapter 3

It was Archie's fault that Perdita and Lettice met.

He had added Lettice's name to Perdita's appeal. Lettice, parsimonious to a point of absurdity, could not be expected to contribute but would enjoy the attention and the giving of reasons for refusal to do so.

She decided to write him a note – heart-rending and quaint.

'Dearest Archie.' There she stopped for a moment to consult a dictionary. 'You know, all too well, of our indigence. What a yoke it is to struggle under. Roland, bless him, has never known of the sacrifices we have made to his art. I feel that one of our sacrifices has to be my contribution to these appeals that you so nobly support.'

Archie asked Harold to finish reading her letter in case any part of it might need a reply.

Lettice wrote to Perdita.

'Dear Mrs Chanter. Who are you, you might ask yourself on receipt of this. And a very fair question that would be! Lettice

Holliday. An old, dear friend of Archie Thorne. He sent me one of your appeals – such a good cause. I gather my poor little daughter-in-law had lunch with you recently. How good of you. I want to thank you somehow. How about a weekend? Soon! End of the month say? Would love it. Lettice Holliday.

'PS: We are covered in a blanket of moss and ivy. Can you bear it? Until then I will be alone here with my husband Roland and my beloved spaniel Orpheus, who lies at my feet as I write. Don't you adore the unquestioning loyalty of dumb animals? I called him Orpheus to remind me of my lute (specially made for me when I was small) and of the celestial poetry of the Bard himself. I think my favourite line in literature is "In sweet Musicke is such Art".'

Perdita, who loathed dogs as did Archie, rang him. 'I couldn't face a weekend of moss and ivy in that dripping part of the world but I've asked her to lunch in London. Now, I suppose, she'll go and accept and bore me rigid quoting Shakespeare. It's all your fault for making me so curious.'

'I refuse to be blamed for your curiosity.'

'Oh, darling. Don't be stuffy. It's living in those lodgings that's made you so gloomy. I shall call them "stuffy lodgings".'

'Very well but cancel lunch with Lettice. It was foolish and unnecessary of you to invite her.'

'How's Tit Widow?'

'Who?'

'Everybody calls her that.'

'What a terribly feeble joke.'

'You can blame Robert Stratton.'

'I must go. I have to dine in hall.'

Perdita decided not to cancel the lunch and booked a table for two at a London restaurant where she was pretty certain to know some of the clientele. Most of the people she knew went there regularly.

She sang:

In those stuffy old lodgings poor Archie now sits,
Singing Widow. Tit Widow. Tit Widow.

Lettice, in mauve, arrived first. Well rehearsed, she embarked immediately.

'It's wonderful to meet somebody on the same wavelength. There are so few kindred spirits in my part of the world.'

Thinking, 'Christ! What a sight!' Perdita dug deep into her bag.

'It was sweet of you to have Victoria to lunch. How did she manage? I've had an agonising time introducing her to our clever friends. You and I have dozens in common, it turns out. Dear Archie's been an angel.'

'Archie? His heart is made of flint.'

Lettice, enraptured by the other's worldliness, had a crack.

'I must admit I can't picture him with wings.'

God, thought Perdita, sipping whisky, something must happen. She twitched her brain as Lettice kept trying.

'What about a halo? Do you think that one would become him?'

Four eyes met. Lettice's teeth were enormous.

Robert Stratton and Victoria came in to the restaurant. Victoria had travelled from the country by train to meet the painter, not realising that Lettice sat alone in her finery in another carriage. Perdita spied them at once.

'Did I invite you both or is it divine coincidence? Sit down and have a glass of whisky while I see to a reshuffle.'

We are the cabinet, Victoria thought, rather wonderful.

She unbuttoned her coat and took it off. Perdita stared at her low-cut dress.

Muscles on Lettice's face, up to then under control, began to run riot – came near to the corner of one eye, gathered and stayed taut for a second before rippling and carrying a tear.

Robert Stratton knew better than to interfere.

'What a delightful party,' Archie passed on his way to a table booked for two, further down the room.

'But I won't join you. I'm in rather a hurry.' He sat and waited for Harold who, on sighting Victoria, had been sick and gone to the lavatory.

Lettice said, 'If this was a novel we'd say it was overdone.'

Perdita whispered, 'Silly, twitching mistress of the obvious remark,' as she turned to Robert. She needed an extra man for a dinner party that night.

Lettice and Victoria caught the same train, free of kindred spirits, back to their part of the world.

That evening Harold wrote some letters.

To Victoria he said, 'I love you very much.'

To Lettice, 'Yours is the only home I have ever known. Why are you not my mother?'

To Perdita, 'I'll never know why I deserve the kindness you show me. Perhaps I am foolish to talk of deserving.'

To Archie, 'I will always be your boy but you must learn to be a more considerate father.'

To the daughter of a colleague, 'Will you marry me, please, at once.' He had only met her twice.

To his own mother, 'You have never been of any use to me at any time.'

He delivered the one for Archie by hand and the others he posted, jerkily, into a private letter box belonging to the college after crediting stamps to an account held by Archie.

He waited until he saw the porter shuffle out with them, walk along the street and wedge them into the stately red box on the corner. Then he ran to his room where he lay, sobbing on his bed, until Archie came to comfort him. Archie rang each member of the letter club, and to each, apart from Harold's mother, he said, 'How shall I put it? Of course it's not nothing to be loved by Harold. You know how sensitive he is. A sensitive genius. He means nothing but good when he writes like that. But of course *à qui vous le dites?* as my predecessor here used to say.'

He rang Harold's mother and said that Harold was sorry for his words but that, of course, he was a genius.

'I don't know about genius.' Mrs Fitch spoke in a flat, drab tone. 'That's for the world to decide. He may have told you that I never cared for him. You should meet Edmund. He's the one that looks to his mother.'

Archie told Harold that his mother had forgiven him and that the others loved him deeply in different fashions although, perhaps, the daughter of his colleague needed time in which to think things over. 'But don't be discouraged.'

Harold said, 'Archie. I will never desert you. Never.' He smashed two ashtrays and a small table.

Victoria answered Harold's letter of love.

'I daresay you asked Archie to mediate. There was no need. I neither take your protestations of love very seriously nor do I ignore them. I hope that suits you. I like you very much although I'm awkward when I'm with you. Perhaps less than at first but your silences can be a bit creepy.'

Harold replied, 'My dear girl. You are very good and I love you more than ever. I am not in love with you. That – being in love with a woman – is a prize to be denied me for ever. I worship you in all the ways I can.'

This correspondence was the only one of the bunch to flourish.

—— Chapter 4 ——

Harold visited Victoria, alone, at the stables and the prize, presumed unattainable, came within his reach although both their needs for Archie remained undiminished. As she thought of Archie and the power he held over her she understood that Harold constituted the only route to intimacy with him. The next best thing. She almost fell for him in a frantic fashion.

Archie sent Victoria a book. 'You are very young,' he wrote. 'This is an interesting book and one which illustrates how many ways there are of loving. You must read it and let me know what you think.'

She read it and considered it a bad example of how to behave.

Harold came again to see her and appeared in her bedroom, crept into her bed and wept with delight; telling her again and again of his early terrors induced by women.

When he returned to Cambridge, he told Archie of his joy.

Archie rang Victoria to say, 'You have made Harold terribly

happy. Aren't you wonderful! I suppose you think I should be jealous. Not at all! It is so frightfully good for him.'

'And for me? Please help me, too.'

'You haul this unique and brilliant creature into your bed and expect me to be sorry for you?'

Later he rang back. 'I was rather unsympathetic. I didn't quite take your point. I'm terribly sorry.'

'That's kind. You are kind. I know you didn't understand but I didn't explain. I could get out of it now, perhaps, but it might be hard later on.'

The weirdness of the passion she had aroused in Harold nearly unhinged her.

'*A qui vous le dites*, as my predecessor used to say. *A qui vous le dites?* My child, how easy it is to say, "Don't worry," but that is my advice. Don't worry and take things as they come.'

She kissed Maudie and decided to drift on. Possibly damage Harold. Assassinate herself. Wound Archie. Take it as it came. Archie was no help. That was for sure. Anxiety for him dissolved.

Perdita said, 'I gather the widow has hauled Harold into her bed. Too macabre. Like interfering with an ostrich.'

Archie, proud of his boy having become a man, basked in lecherous content. His interest in Victoria increased and he wanted to see her alone. He tried to fathom out how to do it without driving Harold wild.

Harold had to go to a family funeral and Archie drove straight to the stables. He took supplies with him and together he and Victoria drank a great deal.

He said, 'Remove that nasty brooch,' and asked her to hold his head and kiss his eyes. 'And now I'd like you to get into my bed.'

In bed, she said, 'I thought something like this might have made you sick. Actually retch.'

'No. I'm not going to be sick – at least I don't think I am. I might be if you don't kiss me at once. You know that I love you.'

'You would be wrong if you didn't.'

'I wish I wasn't so drunk.'

'I'm not rapacious.'

'Don't use such long words. It's terribly confusing.'

'What about Harold?'

'When you're very close to somebody you can't hide things. If I find myself telling him about it I shall let you know immediately.'

He asked her to stay with him. 'Of course I prefer men but with women there are exceptions. I did once go to bed with a woman. She was the wife of a friend of mine. During the war.'

'Was it nice?'

'Not particularly but we have remained friends.'

'That's a relief.'

'Aren't you a goose.'

'Probably.'

'I think you are quite extraordinarily intelligent. Also you deserve a medal. Two medals. I wonder if they are ever awarded for certain services.'

'Do you remember our first meeting?'

'I think you were beside a log fire.'

'I fell in love with you.'

'I know. Quite right. Do you believe now that I love you?' He pulled her on to him. 'I want to grip you between my thighs and I want you to say if you believe I love you. This has nothing to do with Harold. For once he is forgotten. Now. Kiss me again and don't go away. I am terribly old and shall have to go and pee. Stay here and be in my bed when I come back.'

When he returned he wanted to discuss his homosexuality.

'There's something utterly heavenly about queers.' She spoke in high-pitched imitation of Lettice. He told her she had won.

'And, of course, you are frightfully funny. Kiss me again and be quiet. The wonderful thing about this is how little either of us expected it. We didn't have the faintest idea. It's terribly exciting.'

'I never wanted it. I promise I never even thought of it. I only wanted you to love me very much.'

'And now you know that I do. Do you know?' He was rough and he hurt her.

He asked her to tuck him up in bed and leave him.

Later, Harold told her that he always did the same for Archie.

She left him and her moment of advantage was over. It was a terrible wrench. She must return to Harold.

Between the three of them it was decided that Victoria marry Harold. She would have preferred to marry Archie.

Lettice held out her arms. '*Ma belle fille* once more. Harold has always been a son to me.'

Perdita rang Archie. 'Rather bad luck on the widow – pursuing you and ending up as the penniless Mrs Finch.'

'Quite the reverse. I have given them a great deal of money

on the understanding that they take me in as soon as I retire. I have decided to do so earlier than I originally planned. Next week, in fact. In time to join them on their honeymoon.'

'God. What a weird scenario. Where will it take place? The nuptial?'

'At The Old Keep. Lettice has invited us all for a fortnight. Victoria's daughter is, after all, Lettice's granddaughter.'

When, after two years, Roland died, it seemed only fair that Archie should marry Lettice.

Lettice whispered to him as the four sat together in her *denne*, 'I know it's beastly to make conditions. How can I put it? I don't want to hurt you. There is one side – shall I call it the intimate side – to marriage that I must deny you. That belongs to Roland. He had my heart and you shall have my soul. Can you forgive? I would fully understand if it puts you under a strain. I wouldn't even mind if, just occasionally, in London. Not, please, one of the local lasses.'

Archie said, 'My dear girl. You are about to marry a crotchety dotard. Will you change your name to Thorne? Do lettuces have thorns? Perhaps we should re-christen you Rose – rose or blackberry.'

Harold, bored by Archie's incessant need to play with tired words, threw an ornamental gourd at him.

Victoria was sorry for Archie.

'Poor Archie,' she whispered, 'you've drawn the short straw.'

'And the last one,' he whispered in reply. 'Dearest child. Have you ever heard the expression "I can swallow a toad every day"? From now on I shall be called upon to do so.'

Still whispering, she entreated, 'But promise you won't kick Orpheus.'

—— **Chapter 5** ——

They divided their time between The Old Keep and the stables – the 'colleagues' regularly exchanging roles. Harold was besotted with all three of the cast but resentful of the attention commanded by Maudie as she travelled between the domains.

One morning, when Lettice was busy in her *denne* – developing photographs of a dead celebrity – with the words 'Let us now praise famous men' in her best italic handwriting impressed into the picture, Harold, who had spent the night at The Old Keep, wandered over to the stables in search of the company of Archie and Victoria. Nobody was in and doors were locked. No sign, either, of the Daimler that Archie still drove each day although the stables were in walking distance of The Keep.

That morning at breakfast with Victoria, Archie had said, 'Since Maudie is now five and at school all day, let us take an outing together. We could, of course, ask Harold to join us but, well, it would not do to leave Lettice, who is after all my wife, alone with her memories.'

They decided to visit a Bournemouth museum, 'have a bite' somewhere near and get back in time for Maudie's return from school. Victoria rejoiced. These outings with Archie made the whole confusing scheme of the double marriages worthwhile – harrowing though many of the aspects were.

Harold, wearing a rank suit (he owned no country clothes), walked very slowly towards the stables. His hair was long and greasy. He had a severe block about washing it and it fell in damp coils. He believed that his mother had hurt his head when he was small – scrubbing and kneading with a vicious wrist. He had for many years taken an obsessive interest in birds and insects but had always been petrified of women. Until his experiences (few now) with Victoria he had held a fantasy that if he were to touch the breast of a woman it would burst, releasing swarms of wasps, bees and bright bubbles. His mother disliked him and his father was futile in her presence. Victoria had unlocked a dangerous passion in him but her interest had waned, and Harold had soon realised that the arrangement had been agreed to solely through her desire to be near Archie.

Archie, it appeared, worshipped them both although his dislike of Lettice seemed to have increased.

It occurred to Harold that he might murder Victoria. If she were gone, then he, Archie and Maudie could move in with Lettice. Lettice was an admirable grandmother – had even taught herself advanced calligraphy so as to be able to transcribe her favourite poems for Maudie.

But the stables were tightly closed. Every door locked. Jack and Belinda's house, across the way, showed no sign of habitation. He prowled around the place, looking in at windows and testing doors. After picking up a brick, he hurled it at a glass pane above the back door, shattering it. A shard hit his right hand and he extracted one of Archie's spotted handkerchiefs from his pocket to wrap around the wound. Somehow he manoeuvred his body into the building where he snooped into every room reading letters and sifting through Victoria's clothes.

Archie and Victoria returned, having fetched a boisterous Maudie from school gates, to find a shattered glass pane and a few drops of blood by the back door.

'Can it be that some hispid hippy has made an attack on private property?'

'No. No. No. It was me.' Harold advanced clasping Archie's handkerchief to his left wrist. Blood oozed from it.

Violent rappings at the front door. Maudie ran to greet her grandmother who stood in veiled splendour clasping a bunch of exquisitely dried flowers. Maudie seized the bunch and asked, 'Actually, were they expensive?'

Lettice threw up her lace-gloved hands, 'Sainted aunts! What can your dear mother have been teaching you? Our financial position has always been hateful but money plays no part where beauty is concerned. Remember this, Maudie darling.'

Maudie took the flowers to her bedroom and pulled them apart, petal by petal.

Harold wondered if he would, after all, be able to strangle

Victoria now that his wrist was damaged. He knew that he would need two hands for such a job.

After two more years of ups and downs Harold drowned himself in a stagnant pond beyond the garden of The Old Keep.

'The balance of that wonderful mind was undoubtedly disturbed,' Archie repeated over and over again.

Lettice, forgetting which of the two men she had married, lamented, 'Twice widowed. Sainted aunts.'

Archie was never cheerful after the suicide of his beloved 'colleague' and Lettice died, clasping her lute, not long afterwards.

The three Bobbies, and Roland and Lettice's daughters, Alice and Joanna, all moved into The Old Keep – running it as a community centre for artists, which so enraged Archie that he took all his belongings to Victoria at the stables and never ventured again in the direction of The Old Keep. Occasionally he caught sight of a passing community member, usually a long-haired male, whereupon he would snort and utter the words, 'One thing you never see nowadays is the back of a young man's neck.' Victoria got sick to death of hearing it.

Victoria looked after Archie and Maudie as best she could and was happy to have started painting again. Archie's drinking habits had become chronic and life was often tricky and frustrating. However, through Jack and Belinda, she met a merry middle-aged garden designer, a cousin of Belinda, who fell in love with her and, eventually, provided her with a life less confusing than it had been hitherto.

When Archie died of pneumonia combined with alcohol

poisoning, Victoria married the garden designer who proved himself to be an excellent stepfather to Maudie who was on her way to becoming a great beauty.

The End